POTLUCK

C.H. SPRAGUE

SILVER BEECH PRESS

In Rapidan County, Virginia, sheltered by the quiet, self-effacing Blue Ridge, a mountain range less in-your-face than its Rocky cousins to the west or the hot tempered volcanic peaks of the great Northwest, isolation from bustling trade and political shenanigans has fostered a rare climate of cooperative tolerance. People mind their own business for the most part and a live and let live ambience encourages goodwill among men and free thinking among women.

But even in the most placid communities, there are times when emotions run high and some people, in the heat of the moment, take liberties which they otherwise might not. Thus, in the small town of Dudleigh, which nestles between two swelling mountains like an amulet on a full-breasted woman, what passes for social life reaches its apex each year at the annual Fourth of July softball tournament. The tournament began casually, but as years passed rivalries bred like dandelions in the fescue. By the turn of the millenium the tournament had grown to such an extent that the games took place over four days, beginning on July first and culminating in the final on the Fourth. The teams were loose conglomerates of friends, neighbors and families. Sometimes the kids played with the adults at the start of the tournament. But by the time the final came around, the jokes were sharper, the line drives popped like shotgun shells, and the dogs were no longer allowed in the outfield. That's how serious it was.

CHAPTER 1

Denique non omnes eadum mirantur amantque.
All men do not admire and love the same things.
Horace

Possibly the fumes were getting to me, but, honestly, I didn't hear her drive up, and when she slammed the door of her car it sounded like a gunshot, and I guess I must have jumped and lost my grip on the sprayer. That's how my sneakers got drenched with anise extract.

"Duggie?" Jenny was standing in a beam of sunlight, looking more like an angel than usual, which is saying something, since she's pretty spectacular even in the shade. But I could tell by the way she was frowning that she was already writing me up in her log for another infraction of the crazy code.

"What are you doing? And what is that smell? Are you smoking Good and Plenty now?"

I smiled in my winning way and said, "I know this looks funny, but this is key to the success of my venture."

"You mean your crop?"

"Shhhh!" I hissed, swiveling my glance to the woods behind us.

"Oh come on. Who's going to hear us out here?"

I didn't respond to this, not wanting to get into it. Jenny doesn't smoke pot, didn't even in high school, on account of being serious about athletics, so she doesn't get the whole walls-have-ears paranoia thing. Even if there aren't walls, which, of course, there aren't around the bus. Still.

"Yes, I know. Miles from everywhere. It's a matter of principle." I leaned my head closer to hers and said, *sotto voce*, "We don't discuss it."

She kind of sniffed and said, "So what are you doing, anyway? Playing *Ghostbusters*?"

In reference to my mask and the tank of odorous spray, I explained that the idea was to spray the outside of the bus so that if pot sniffing dogs were sent to find my crop, they would be completely misled by the powerful reek of anise. I read about it in a Terry Pratchett novel as a way to discourage werewolves, and it seemed like a good idea. Not that I'm expecting any werewolves, but you can never be too careful.

Jenny shrugged. "Okay. I guess you're not completely nuts."

"Oh, I don't know about that."

She smiled, causing me to shoot another pint of spray on my shoe.

"Are you okay?" she asked, as I shook the sodden footwear.

"Yeah. Yeah, I'm good. What brings you here, anyway?"

Her smile went behind a cloud, and she did that thing where she stares at the ground and chews her lower lip, like she used to in high school when she was getting ready to say no after I'd asked her out for the millionth time.

I should mention that the torch I have carried for Jenny Carson has been burning longer than those tire fires in Ohio that blight the lives of the locals. I fell in love with her when I was a senior at Fairfax High School, and she was an incoming freshman. She never took me seriously then, and continued to blow me off after college and in the wayward years that followed when I would try to convince her that I had matured. During all this time, of course, she has had numerous swains falling at her feet and offering diamonds and pearls, convertibles and ranch houses, the customary swag of the marital rites, but, for some reason, she has turned them all down, and we're still friends. I don't understand it; I no longer even try. Jenny is the sun and I revolve around her. She doesn't know. She thinks I'm still looking for a girlfriend. I let her think that because I don't want to be a pest.

The truth is, I stopped looking long ago. Well, not looking. I am human. But I don't bother going out with them anymore. I used to. I'd meet a girl, and she'd seem nice, and we'd have a few laughs. And then she'd start wanting to get serious, and she wouldn't be Jenny. And that was always the thing. It's like, Jenny's the gold standard, and those other women, they might be silver, or platinum or titanium. It doesn't matter. I'm doomed.

But it's okay, because Jenny's happy the way things are, with us just being really close friends. So when she stops smiling, I do too.

"Duggie ..."

"What?"

She did the lip chewing thing again, and I began to worry that she had met someone.

"You know the game's coming."

This wasn't a question, because we both knew what game she was talking about. It was the beginning of June, after all, which meant that the Fourth of July tournament was coming up. In other parts of the country, fireworks provide the holiday excitement, but in Rapidan the high point of the Independence celebration is the softball tournament, which used to be one game on the Fourth but has grown into a four-day event that gets everybody going, whether they play or not. My big sister Glory runs the Moonlight Café in town, and she always sponsors a team. Jenny and I always play on it. Jenny's the pitcher, because she's great at it, having played in high school and in college.

She looked at me with the smile switched off, and I felt the way I always do when she turns those dark brown eyes on me full blast. Think stun gun.

"It's Shipley."

"Who?"

"Shipley. My boss?"

"At the Swan?"

"Right."

"The stuffy twit who hates softball?"

"Right."

"What about him?"

She took a deep breath, and I wobbled a bit but didn't let on.

"He's decided he's going to sponsor a team this year, and he wants me to be in charge."

"What?" I goggled at her for a minute, wondering if the fumes had gotten to me after all. "You can't be on his team. You're always on our team."

"I know. I told him. But he said I have to do it or look for another job."

I should perhaps explain that Jenny works as a waitress at The Black Swan, the snooty restaurant in town, the place that drives my sister mad with envy because they have a four-star rating in the Washington, D.C., area dining guide, even though they're more than an hour outside the beltway. Ever since that rating came out the Swan has been lording it over the local scene. They raised their prices and swanked up their menu, and Glory has been losing sleep over how to compete. She recently went on a recruiting mission to New York and brought back this amazing Cuban chef, and since he's been around Glory has been a lot more optimistic. But she loves the softball tournament, and it's always been a point of pride with her that the Moonlighters participate in it. This Swan owner has previously turned up his nose at the tournament, claiming once, in an interview, that softball was a pastime for boors.

"I don't want to have to look for another job. There's no place else I could make the kind of money I make at the Swan."

I saw her point. The tips at the Swan come from a different tax bracket than the ones that trickle out at the Moonlight Café. Glory's hoping to get more upscale, but the change will take time, and there really isn't any place else for Jenny to work unless she goes back to teaching, which she quit before because she couldn't live on the crappy pay.

While we had been standing there a festive multitude of gnats had gathered in the air about us, perhaps getting high on the anise. Jenny wiped one out of her eye and said, "I've got to get away from this smell. I think I'm gonna need a shower." She shrugged. "I'm sorry. You know I'd rather play with the Moonlighters."

"I understand. We'll figure something out."

After she'd gone I finished up the spraying, but my heart wasn't in it. I kept thinking about how weird it was going to be to play in the tournament and have to play against Jenny. I didn't want to lose, but I didn't want her to lose, but I didn't want Shipley to win either.

Normally, when the confusion gets this bad, I head over to Morris's, knowing that I can count on him to help me slay the dragons and find the talisman and make it to the next level. But lately things have been a little tense between us, because Morris is dead set against the pot bus. I tried to explain to him how it was a sure thing, a simple money-making enterprise that couldn't fail. I have a buyer already lined up for the product. I completely sealed the bus from view, and with the high current lights and enhanced liqui-drip feeding system my two hundred sensimilla plants will be ready to harvest by the end of July, leaving me with a tidy profit to invest in my bookstore plan.

Morris, usually unflappable, refused to encourage me. "Entangled folly brings humiliation," he said, in that inscrutable 'wisdom of the Orient' way of his, which, let's be honest, can get a bit tiresome. I mean, if you were lost on the way to somewhere, and you needed directions, possibly Morris would be willing to be less opaque. I wouldn't count on it.

I think it comes from being a mystery writer. Morris writes bestsellers. You've probably never heard of him, because he writes everything under his pen name, Daphne Murdock. Now you've heard of him, huh? And trust me, Morris is fantastic. He'd be my best friend, except he's kind of too smart for that. Also, he's older, in his fifties, and he kind of likes being left alone. It's part of that writing thing. He used to be married, but after he got divorced he came up here from Charlottesville. That's where I met him, at UVA, when I took a class in creative writing as an elective because I thought it would be easy. Man, was that a mistake. Luckily, Morris took pity on me and let me pass. We became friends after that, and when I found out that he'd bought a place up the mountain from me it was perfect. Like having Buddha move in up the street. Except a more talkative Buddha who spoke English.

You'd think Buddha would like pot, though, wouldn't you? Morris does, but he won't admit it. He mostly drinks wine. He says pot just adds to the confusion. Maybe he's right. I wouldn't know. I'm too confused. Hah.

However, once I got out of the licorice scented shoes, I couldn't deny that the loss of Jenny on the team was a blow. And not just because she's the woman I love. She's also got a right arm that can smoke them over the plate at seventy miles per hour, which would be fast for a normal guy. For a girl, well, let's just say the batter who gets a hit off Jenny feels an unusual sense of accomplishment.

I knew we would be able to field a team without her. But I didn't know how Glory was going to take it when she found out that Jenny had gone over to play for the Dark Side. I figured I better tell her sooner, rather than later, because, in my experience, these things you worry about are never the ones that bite you in the ass. The ones you should be worried about are the ones you don't see coming, except how could you if you have no clue? And besides, worry never helps anything, so I figure, why bother? We could all be dead tomorrow, right? Might as well *carpe diem*.

I headed in to work and found Glory in the kitchen up to her elbows in arugula. When people see me next to my sister they often look skeptical of our shared heritage, since my sister is, let's say, formidable—no stinting on the portions, I mean—while my physique might best be described as standard geek, more brain tissue than muscle mass. We both have the same hazel eyes, and Glory's brightened when she saw me. I was glad to see she was in good spirits. But then she said, in that peremptory way of hers when the luncheon fray is near and the troops aren't marching quickly enough to suit her plans, "Hey, get over here and start washing this arugula, would you? Rosalie is late and Eduardo is already muttering and I've got a hundred things to do."

"Rosalie is late?" This was odd, since our ravishing French kitchen intern was a model of punctual efficiency.

Glory leaned her head closer to mine, and I could see the concern in her eyes as she whispered, "I'm afraid she's trying to avoid Eduardo. I think when they're alone in the kitchen together he's been hovering."

"Hovering?"

She glanced around to make sure he wasn't listening. "Yes. He's got the hots for her, and she doesn't want to offend him, but she's really not interested."

"You know this for a fact?"

"She confided in me last weekend. I told her to tell him she had a fiancé back in France, but she doesn't want to lie. Go figure."

I nodded sympathetically. These kitchen romances are hell for Glory. She says it's one of the risks of the job. You put two people in a steamy room and turn up the pressure, and things just happen. With Eduardo, the stakes are higher. Glory has had chefs quit over disagreements before, but a chef like Eduardo isn't easy to replace. The guy can do things with chicken and tomatoes that you wouldn't think possible. And if chocolate's involved, all bets are off.

"Want me to talk to her?" I have a way with the ladies, it's well known.

Glory looked at me warily. "You think that would help?"

"Could it hurt?" I responded sunnily.

She frowned. "Fine. But whatever you do, don't hit on her, okay? I think every guy she's met since she got here has asked her out within five minutes, and she's starting to get a little gun shy."

"Never fear. My heart belongs to another. Speaking of which, or whom, rather, I have some bad news about the team."

A look of alarm darted across Glory's face. "What?"

"Jenny can't play for us."

Glory's alarmed look reversed course and slowed to a saunter. "Jeez. Are you trying to get me worked up? I thought you said it was bad news."

"It is. She's the best pitcher in the county."

"So? Pitching isn't everything. Why can't she play anyway? Did you annoy her?"

"Hardly. She's feeling really bad about letting us down, actually. But Shipley's put the squeeze on her. He says she's got to play for him or get fired."

Glory froze, a look of horror on her face, as if she'd discovered a hairy wolf spider nesting in the arugula. "Shipley's entering the tournament?"

"Apparently. Jenny says he wants her to put together a crack team."

"That bastard." Glory started tossing the greens in a way that would have been life threatening if they hadn't already been dead.

"You know why he's doing this?" she snapped.

I shrugged. I hadn't given it a thought.

"It's obvious! He's been snooping around about Eduardo, trying to find a talking point."

"Really? And he's hoping that talking sports will give him a leg up?"

"No, you idiot. He's found out about Eduardo's hitting."

I raised my eyebrows. This was news to me. "Is Eduardo a hitter?"

Glory snorted. "He's Cal Ripken with a mustache. He's Babe Ruth with an accent. He's Manny Ramirez without the attitude. He loves baseball. When I told him we had a softball team at the restaurant, his eyes lit up like a little kid's. I think it's what sealed the deal. I know Shipley's already offered him more money to work for him, but so far Eduardo's been loyal, and I don't know whether it's because of Rosalie or the team or both, but all I know is that if Shipley's putting together a team, he's only doing it to try to steal Eduardo."

I nodded sympathetically. "Wow. I had no idea."

"Well now you see why we have to win this tournament. I stand a better chance of keeping Eduardo if we're the number one team. He won't want to join a bunch of losers."

"Even if they're four-star-rated losers?"

"We're going to get another star."

"Really?"

"With Eduardo in the kitchen, it's only a matter of time. The next reviewer who comes here is going to notice. You watch. Now get to work."

I saluted and went out to the bar to get things in order for the lunch crowd. This Moonlight Café of my sister's has come a long way since she took it over five years ago, when her marriage went kablooey. She invested her portion of the settlement in a rambling old house and the Moonshine Diner, which sat more or less in the front yard of the house, right on the main road into Dudleigh. Glory changed the name to Moonlight Café and started out serving lunch and dinner in the old diner. She did well, and gradually expanded the business into the house. She hired some architects to design and build a connecting wing, with lots of windows and charm, and the whole thing kind of took off. Now she's got three stars in the local restaurant guide, but she yearns for that fourth star like a bald man yearns for hair. So I could understand why she was worried about the possibility of Shipley stealing her chef.

The thing of it is, Shipley's got a big league chef already, a guy who's written a bestselling cookbook and everything. But I guess these restaurateurs don't like to leave anything to chance. They're like movie stars—they don't want to be upstaged by anyone.

This Shipley dude, Prentice is his name, though everyone in the county calls him Shitley behind his back, came from out of nowhere about ten years ago and completely remodeled a historic old house in the heart of Dudleigh, pissing off the preservationist types no small amount, and then he staffed the place with a small army of outsiders, claiming, word has it, that the locals weren't couth enough to provide the kind of service his clientele would demand. And then he posted a menu with prices that guaranteed no locals could afford to eat there. So, all in all, not a guy way into the whole 'giving back to the community' thing. The only thing he has ever given the community is a boatload of crap about the town's restrictions on his parking lot.

And now this guy wants to be a spoiler in the community softball tournament? I don't think so, Shitley. I don't think so.

CHAPTER 2

secretum iter et fallentis semita vitae
a quiet journey in the untrodden path of life
Horace

A degree in classical languages prepares you to do one of three
things: teach, write, or wait tables.

Customers sometimes ask me why I'm not working in a
classroom, or writing some scholarly text, and I always tell them
that, like Bartleby, I'd prefer not to.

It's depressing how few of them have ever heard of Bartleby.
You know who I mean, right? The Melville anti-hero who declined
the glory of honest labor? Not that there's anything wrong with it.
Honest labor, I mean. I'm all for it. It's the phony labor that irks
me. Like spending fifty hours a week pounding Latin verbs into
kids who would rather be NASCAR drivers than lawyers anyway,
so, I say, why bother? Let them study fuel transmission or
whatever. Why should I torture them with Tacitus?

I bet, if you did the numbers, there's not one kid in a thousand
who really enjoys studying Latin. I was that kid. And let me tell

you, high school is not designed for kids like me. I got through it by pretending to be somebody else, by blaming my brains on my parents, hiding the pleasure I found in reading the Stoics. But, now, looking back at the years I spent after college when I was still trying to pass on the wisdom of the ancients, I realize what an ass my students must have thought me.

And I see now that they weren't all wrong. And I hope, wherever they are, whatever they're doing, be it producing hip hop videos in Los Angeles or changing tires in Indianapolis, that they are happy. Because, *vita brevis*—life is short, as Hippocrates said. Actually, he said "Life is short, art is long, opportunity fleeting, experience treacherous, judgment difficult." But not many people care. Which is why I don't bother them with it anymore. The way I've got it figured now is, the world is screwed up, but it's not my fault, and, more importantly, I am not the kind of live-large, take-charge guy who can fix it. The best I can do, I honestly believe, is not make things worse. So my current goal in life is to lay low. Possibly open a small bookstore. Someplace I can sell a few books, read when there aren't customers. Not in the city. Right here. In Rapidan, where nobody drives fast and nobody cares what you wear.

That's a good thing, because, on the money I make bartending and bussing tables for Glory, I can barely afford to pay the electric bill at my shack. Shopping at The Gap is out of the question. Luckily I get to eat a lot of leftovers at the café, so I can pretty much survive without much dough.

And life is good. But it will be even better when my sensimilla crop is harvested and sold to the dealer from Charlottesville who promised me a five figure payoff on delivery, which should be by the end of August. The plants are so bushy now I can hardly walk down the aisle of the bus to water them without getting a contact high. Some of them are touching the roof of the bus. More importantly, they're starting to bud, so it won't be long now.

I admit, despite my bravado when Morris is around, it will be a relief when this is all over. I know some guys get off on the rush of illegality, but I could do without it. Even though I don't think pot should be illegal, obviously, and I wish the FDA wasn't completely owned by the tobacco and alcohol industries, who are the real reason weed will never be legal in this country, I still don't feel entirely at ease with this whole venture, only because I know how badly the cops around here would love to make a major bust.

So I'm always a little on edge when I'm taking care of the plants. Which is why I nearly hit my head on the roof of the bus when Eric yelled "Hah!"

I turned the hose on him to wipe the grin off his face.

"Okay, okay," he said, shielding his face from the water.

I switched off the hose. "Are you trying to give me a heart attack?"

"You're too young for a heart attack." Eric replied, but, I noticed, for I'm a pretty perceptive guy even when my heart is racing, that he seemed to have something on his mind.

"What are you doing here? I thought you were going to avoid the scene of the crime." Eric, like Morris, advised against the pot bus from the get-go. However, unlike Morris, Eric doesn't have the credentials to make his advice worth heeding. I mean, he's a guy with a degree in English who works as a contractor, because he gave up after his girlfriend dumped him for her professor. Now Eric is cynical about the entire academic process. He claims there's more integrity in building houses. I wouldn't know, but Eric's a good guy. We were in high school together.

He sighed loudly. Then he shook his head and said, "Can we talk outside the bus? The air in here is kind of ..."

"Yeah, it's kind of intense." I followed him out of the bus. We went over to the folding chairs under the tree in front of my shack. The night air was really warm considering it wasn't even July yet, and the fireflies were breakdancing in the bushes.

I pulled out the shoebox of dope from the trash can beside the door. "Want a joint?" I asked, ever the courteous host.

"Sure." Eric waited until I had rolled the reefer, and we had both had a few tokes, before he spoke again.

"She makes me feel stupid."

He didn't have to tell me who 'she' was. Ever since he laid eyes on Amanda Carson, Jenny's little sister, Eric has been unable to think or talk about anyone else. On the plus side, this is great because he's no longer moping about Kirsten, his former girlfriend, the one he'd been dating since high school. They had been planning on marriage, the house, the two-point-five kids, the whole deal, before she dumped him. But, although Eric has been unable to talk about anything but Amanda since he first saw her behind the counter at the diner, he has yet to say one word to her. He says he goes in there every day planning to ask her out, and winds up only leaving a big tip. I told him this was not a bad way to initiate a relationship with a girl, since it lets her see you as a generous, thoughtful person, before she's found out you're really a selfish animal like every other guy. Except me, of course. Thoughtful to the core.

"How? Does she ask you trick questions?" I replied.

"Of course not. We haven't spoken yet." He inhaled deeply, coughed, and then began again. "I go in there and I have two or three lines ready."

"About what?"

"You know. The weather. The, um, weather." He frowned into the darkness. "I've got to start somewhere."

I nodded encouragingly. "You could ask her about herself. Where she's from. Is she in school? That kind of thing."

"I know all about her. I talked to Jenny. She told me how Amanda had this boyfriend who wasn't good enough for her, and now she's just regrouping before she goes away again. I don't have much time."

I smiled patiently. These romantic English majors are all the same. They see love as this desperate drama. Whereas from my perspective it's more like a musical comedy. First act, boy meets girl, Marvin Gaye—*Let's Get it On*. Second act, misunderstandings, complications, Smokey Robinson—*Tears of a Clown*. Third act, kiss and make up, Van Morrison—*Warm Love*.

I think the reason most people have problems is they're not listening to the right soundtrack. It's all there. You just have to follow the notes, stay with the rhythm, have faith in the beat. You don't even need to remember all the words. Everyone knows the important ones.

So this is what I tell Eric, but he only shakes his head, muttering about Doyle Krump.

This Doyle Krump was Amanda's former boyfriend, and from what Jenny tells me, he's not totally out of the picture yet. The break up happened a few months ago, when Amanda and DK were driving to the beach for her spring break and apparently they got in some sort of argument, and in the course of it Amanda threw DK's suitcase out the window onto the highway. Well, you can see how that might spoil the mood. Luckily, they were able to get the suitcase back, and it wasn't hit by a car or anything. But, unluckily, unknown to Amanda, DK had packed a couple of bottles of wine among his clothes, and these broke, completely ruining his entire wardrobe for the vacation.

Still, you might argue that if the relationship had been a good one they could have put this little episode in the past, perhaps even laughing about it with their grandchildren one day. But DK is more of the brooding, scorekeeping type. He kept bringing it up, reminding Amanda of this or that shirt or favorite pair of pants that were gone forever thanks to her, and, eventually, she decided to join their ranks.

Personally, I think she's well rid of an oaf like DK. He was a successful jock in high school, and though he no longer wears the letter jacket, he carries himself with the same swaggering self-satisfaction despite the fact that he now works for a Ford dealership in Manassas. Amanda can do better. She's studying to be a graphic designer and has all this artistic ability.

"Why don't you ask her to design some business cards for you?"

Eric sat up straighter. "You think she'd do that?"

"Does it matter? You don't need business cards. But she's good at design. It would give you something to talk about—to get the ball rolling."

Eric nodded. "You know, that's not a bad idea. I can definitely do that."

I smiled. "Glad to help."

We sat for a few minutes in the dark, listening to the locusts buzzing in the woods. Every so often some bird joined in with a few blues lines, but nothing in the way of actual music. Still, it was peaceful. Some might say dull.

Eric was apparently one of them, as he jumped up after a few moments and said, "I might as well go."

"Hey, don't forget practice tomorrow."

"Since when do we practice?"

"Since Jenny quit the team."

Eric dropped back in his chair as if he'd been shot. "What? Jenny quit the team?"

"Shitley forced her. He's entering a team in the tournament, and he told her she has to play for him or get fired."

Eric's mouth hung open, but he seemed to be at a loss for words. I completely sympathized, of course. I had been puzzling over the pitching dilemma all day at work and still hadn't found anything close to a solution.

"Who's going to pitch for us?" he managed, finally.

"I don't know. That's why we need to have a practice. We've got to find someone."

"There isn't anyone ..."

We both paused, I think because neither one of us wanted to finish that statement. But, we both knew what went in the blank.

"Unless ..."

"I guess if we're really desperate ..."

"Darren?" Eric whispered, as if he thought the kid might be listening in the woods and would come bounding out with a whoop and a wild gleam in his eye.

"Yeah, well. He has got an arm," I said.

"Too bad he hasn't got a brain."

I shook my head. "He's not dumb. He's just a little ..."

"Insane?"

I shrugged. "Possibly. But in a good way."

"Right." Eric snorted derisively. "If Darren pitches we'll need to get some helmets."

I nodded. "Maybe so. But who else have we got? You? Me? Witty?" I didn't bother to run through the whole roster of regulars who played for the Moonlighters. We both knew there was no one among them who could come close to filling Jenny's shoes. The thing about Darren is, he's a real Rapidan kid. Born and raised here, not like all of us who migrated from the suburbs of D.C. Darren's like some wild mustang running loose in the fields where the fat pony ring veterans spend their days eating sweet grass and swishing flies with their tails. Nobody knows what Darren does with his time, but he can always find weed if you want it. And the only person who can get his attention is his older sister Natalie, who works at the bowling alley.

I've never understood why Darren has played for the Moonlighters in the past. He can't hit, and he plays in the deep outfield where the balls rarely fly, so he spends most of the game swatting at gnats. I've never thought about it much until today, when I was wracking my brains trying to come up with somebody and the only person that came to mind was Darren Stark and his long arms, flailing like a turbocharged pinwheel.

I found Darren at the Bust-a-Gut. He was playing Doom Warrior in the game room and didn't hear me walk in. His face, glowing green and blue in the reflected light of the game, had the kind of intensity you usually see only in samurai movies right before the master swordsman slices up a dozen attackers who, unlike everybody else in the entire movie, aren't aware of the guy's blinding skills.

"Darren?" I said softly, not wanting to break his concentration, but apparently not loud enough to be heard above the virtual carnage. "Darren?" I said louder. He twitched, like a samurai giving the foolhardy attackers one last chance to get out of Dodge. I took a step back and said "Darren" again, but staying on my toes in case a further retreat appeared prudent.

His eyes stayed locked on the game but he said, "What?" in a voice that managed to convey both boredom and contempt in equal measure.

"It's me. Duggie. I need to talk to you about the game."

"Wait. Just let me finish killing these guys."

"Sure. Sure. Take your time. I'll just sit here." I looked around, but, of course, there weren't any chairs in the game room. Nobody sits down to play an arcade game. You have to stand up to show the game who's boss. I leaned against a machine and waited while Darren completed his massacre. When his shoulders finally relaxed, and the last screams died out from the machine, he turned to me and said, in a tone 180 degrees west of his game face, "Dugggieee. What's up?"

"It's about the game."

"The softball game?"

"Yeah."

Darren shrugged. "I'm playing, right? Is that what you wanna know?"

"Um, no. I was counting on you to play. But ... now ..." I took a deep breath and nearly choked on the residual microwaved popcorn aroma. "Well, the thing is, this situation has um ... come up. And Jenny's not gonna be able to play for us this year."

"Bummer. She's hot."

I frowned. "Yeah. She's hot. That's not the point. The point is, we don't have a pitcher." I waited to see him connect the dots, but his face remained blank. "So we need to find someone on the team who can pitch, and we thought of you."

Darren's eyebrows lifted a fraction, as if I had just slain some virtual opponent in a particularly unexpected manner. "Dude. You joking?"

"No. You've got a good arm. Have you ever pitched?"

"Not since Little League." He snickered. "That didn't work out so good."

"Why not?"

"Hit some kid. Broke his arm. His parents wanted to sue me."

"Did they?"

"Natalie talked 'em down. But I quit the team. Too many rules."

I nodded. Rapidan kids don't place too high a value on regulation, especially in matters of recreation. "I hear you. But you won't have to worry about rules with us. You know how we play. We just need somebody who can pitch. How about it?"

Darren started swaying on his heels, back and forth. I could tell he was weighing the pros and cons. I decided to sweeten the pot, so to speak. "I'll give you twenty bucks to play."

"Oh yeah? Well, cool. Done and done, man."

"Don't tell anyone I'm paying you, okay? I can't pay everybody."

Darren nodded. "Got it. No problem."

"So we have a deal?"

He grinned. I knew what he would say next.

"Sure. How about an advance? Say ten bucks?"

I grimaced but coughed up, reminding myself as the fellow said that *nil posse creari de nilo*. Nothing can be created out of nothing.

I left after telling him about practice. He seemed enthusiastic. And so infectious was his enthusiasm that I had driven halfway up the mountain to my shack before it occurred to me that a pitcher, no matter how wild, needs a catcher in order to do his best for the team. Jenny always worked with Babe McLaren. But now, with Jenny playing for the Swan, would Babe leave us as well?

Babe is what you might call a woman of substance. She runs a landscaping business. She has a crew of Mexicans who work for her. She can parallel park a backhoe. Her real name is Bridget, but in high school she went out a few times with a guy named Paul Hardy, and some class clown took the opportunity to mock her super-size proportions by calling her Babe the Blue Ox. By the time his cast came off he had seen the error of his ways, but Babe had come to embrace the nickname. She absorbed it, like The Hulk, and it only made her stronger.

I knew that Babe's loyalty to Jenny was greater than her feelings for the Moonlighters. I hoped she'd stick with our team anyway. The minute she answered the phone I could tell she'd already made up her mind.

"Sorry, Duggie. I'd like to help you guys out. But, you know, Jenny asked me to play for the Swans, and you know, me and Jenny ... well ... if Jenny's pitching, I'm catching. That's pretty much the way it is."

I knew that, of course, but I had a shot at appealing to her team loyalty. It didn't get very far, mostly I think because Babe and Glory have never been exactly on the same page, what with Babe being all about social justice and workers' rights, and Glory being more focused on bottom line issues. They get along okay. They don't hang out together.

I hung up the phone and stared out the window for a while. I considered walking over to Morris's, on the chance that he might have some useful suggestion. But I hesitated. He's been holding back ever since I went ahead with the pot bus, like he's waiting for me to screw up so he can say nothing because he'll know that I know what he's not saying. And even though everything is going according to plan and I know he's wrong, I'd rather not ask his advice until I've proven I'm not the idiot he thinks I am for going ahead with the bus. So I decided to do the next best thing. I got out the old box and rolled a personal-pan-sized joint and fired it up.

Almost immediately I had an idea. I got a piece of paper and made a list of the players on our team. There was me, Eduardo, Darren, Eric, Witt, Photon, Randall, Amanda and ... I sat there for a while, waiting for the last name to come to me. After a while I decided some food might help me think so I went to the cupboard and found a box of crackers. After eating six or seven I got thirsty, so I went to the refrigerator and got a beer. Then I stared some more at the list waiting for inspiration.

The trouble is, most everybody in Dudleigh who plays ball is already on a team. And that was before Shipley started raiding players. The firehouse always has a team. Some of them are kind of over the hill, and more out of shape than me, but most of them played ball back in high school, and they still know how to play. But I couldn't get any of them to play for us. The firefighters are all guys, and they don't think much of our team having girls, except for Jenny and Babe, of course, and now we don't even have them.

I was starting to feel a little discouraged when an owl hooted outside and I had a flash of brilliance. It all came to me at once. If I could persuade Witt to be the catcher, I could put Photon in his spot in center field, and I could get Rosalie to play right field. Of course, I didn't know if Rosalie knew how to play softball. Probably not, what with being French and all. But it wouldn't matter, really, because Photon could come over from center field and cover for her. Rosalie would definitely be an asset, if only as a distraction to the other team.

In real baseball this wouldn't work of course. But in our league, where half the guys, no, probably more like ninety percent of the guys out there are either single or wish they were, the chance to ogle a woman like Rosalie in the flesh doesn't come often. And even though I'd never seen her in shorts and a tank top, I had a feeling that the sight would prove irresistible to some of our competition.

Plus, I reasoned, Eduardo might like having Rosalie on the team, since then they'd have something else in common besides working in the kitchen. Dimly I seemed to recall Glory saying something about Rosalie being freaked by Eduardo's attention, but I dismissed this. The important thing was to get a full team on the field, and now I saw the way.

I rolled another joint to celebrate.

The next day when I got to work I found Rosalie in the kitchen rubbing herbs into some poultry. Eduardo was on the other side of the room manning a vat of soup. The whole room smelled fantastic. It made me wish I'd eaten breakfast before I came, but there's never anything in my house that looks edible in the morning.

Rosalie looked up and smiled, and I felt a spasm of lust. Instantly doused, of course, by my pure devotion to Jenny. But still, in a purely clinical, scientific way, you can't help but notice that when it comes to looks Rosalie is like some goddess who accidentally wound up in our mortal dimension. Or maybe she pissed off one of the higher gods and got sent here for community service. Anyway, I shook it off and went into my spiel.

"Good morning," I began.

"Bonjour," she said.

"Rosalie, I need to ask you to do me a favor. It's not really for me. You'd be helping Glory too, and the restaurant."

She tilted her head and lifted her eyebrows, and I wondered if I was going too fast for her. Her English isn't that great. She and Eduardo kind of communicate in bits and pieces of French and Spanish and English. Considering this, it's amazing the food turns out so well, I guess.

"Favor?" she said. "Like, um, for party?"

I shook my head rapidly. "No, no. Por favor. To help me?"

"You need help?" A smile flickered briefly on her face, and I wondered if she'd picked up on my sister's attitude.

"The softball team needs your help. We lost two of our players and we need to find someone to play right field. You wouldn't have to do anything really. You just have to stand out in the field while the other team is at bat, and if they hit a ball toward you, Photon will get it."

She frowned slightly. "I don't understand. If I do nothing, why be on the team?"

"The team has to have nine players. That's the way it works. And, you'll get to bat when we have our innings. But you don't have to worry about that. Nobody will expect you to hit the ball."

She frowned again. "You don't think I can make a hit?"

"No, no. That's not what I mean. I mean, there would be no pressure on you. Nobody would expect you to hit homers or anything. We just want you to be on our team. It will be fun. I promise. Please say you'll do it."

"When is the game?"

"There's actually three games. It's a tournament. Everybody plays everybody, and then the top two teams play a final on the Fourth of July."

"So maybe four games?"

I nodded and smiled. "Right. If we get lucky, it could be four games."

She finished messing with the poultry and washed her hands before she spoke. I jumped in and started washing her dishes, figuring every little bit helps. She looked at me and her mouth twisted in a funny way that I can only say seemed very French to me. Then she wiped her hands on a towel and said, "Okay. I do it. Maybe I surprise you."

"Really! That's great! Thank you. Glory will be really glad. Everybody will be glad. You'll have fun."

"Doogie. I said I do it."

I reined in the enthusiasm. "Right. Great. Um. We're going to have a short practice this afternoon. Before the dinner shift. If you want to come. You don't have to. We'll just be working in our new pitcher."

"Okay. Where?"

I told her how to get to the Ruritan field. By the time I was setting up tables out front my entire mental outlook had taken a turn for the better. There was definitely a chance that we might win a game if Eduardo was half as good as Glory said he was. And with Rosalie on our team, he'd be even more motivated, right? There was no downside to this picture. I whistled a medley of Jimmy Buffet tunes while I worked. Until Glory came out from her office and told me to can it. Some people have no romance in their souls.

Chapter 3

Vis unita fortior.
Force is increased by union.

When I got to the field a few hours later, Darren was standing by himself tossing a ball up in the air and catching it. He looked at me and said, "Where is everybody?"

"Oh, they'll be along. We don't usually practice at all, you know, so this is kind of optional."

"So I can go?"

"No. You're the reason we're here."

Darren smirked. "Countin' on me huh?"

"Yeah, well. Let's see how you pitch." I got out my glove slowly, hoping someone else would show up before I had to fill in as catcher. I can't take all that squatting. Kills my knees.

A deep roar like the throaty growl of a pack of Harleys burst onto the field, and Witty's Chevy lurched to a halt in a cloud of dust. He got out and slammed the door shut, emerging from the dust like some old style cowpoke arriving in town after a long trail ride.

"Heyoh," he called as he ambled over. The 'smock smock' sound of him smacking his fist into his glove echoed in the stillness. He looked around the empty field and said, "This all we got?"

"I told everyone it wasn't mandatory practice."

"How come you didn't tell me? I left work for this."

I took a deep breath and said, "Did you hear about Jenny?"

Witt's scowl deepened. "Some fool told me she quit the team. He was lying, right?"

I took another deep one. Unfortunately a gnat rode in with it, and it took me a couple of minutes to stop coughing. When I did, I told Witt of the latest developments re Shipley and the Swan team.

"Son of a bitch," Witt said, when I finished. He looked at Darren, who had been lounging against a tree this whole time. "Well, I guess I can be catcher. Let's see if you can pitch."

Before Darren got as far as the mound, another car drove up, its engine purring like a sewing machine. It came to halt next to my truck. The door popped open, and Rosalie stepped out, wearing a tight purple tank top and cut-off jeans, looking just like she did in my fantasies.

"Hi," I called.

She smiled and waved. Her dark hair was pulled back in a ponytail that fell to the middle of her back. She was wearing sandals. I wondered if she even owned any sneakers. I turned to introduce her to Witty, but when I saw his face I realized the damage was done. He was already beyond caring what her name was.

I met Bob "Witty" Whitmore at UVA when we both had to take Rocks 101 for our science credit. One day when we happened to be sitting next to each other in a lecture hall the size of a football field, we realized there was no need for both of us to be there all the time if we shared notes. So we devised a system where we alternated attendance, which worked great since the professors in those big intro courses don't care if you come or not.

Witty got into UVA on a wrestling scholarship, and he had no idea what he wanted to do when he got out of college. But the one thing he believed, with a faith that was unshakable, was that his life would be meaningless unless he shared it with the right woman. In the time that I've known him, the search for this woman has led Witty into and out of some of the most bizarre relationships I've ever witnessed, but despite all his wrong turns and lost girlfriends, Bob Whitmore still falls in love at first sight with a regularity that is nothing short of awe-inspiring. And, I could see at a glance that one look at Rosalie had done the trick.

Naturally, I couldn't blame him in this case. I mean, if I weren't already locked and loaded for Jenny, I could easily imagine myself with a luscious babe like Rosalie. In fact, as I mentioned earlier, I have entertained a few idle daydreams while washing dishes at the café. I blame it on the hot water. You stand there for hours with your hands all wet and warm, and your brain kind of drifts. That's probably what got all those soap operas started. But I digress. The point is, what with Rosalie being the kind of woman that any normal guy would be happy to daydream about, and Witty being a guy who could qualify for the Olympics if they had a lover's leap event, it didn't take a genius to see the approaching heartbreak.

I say heartbreak because, for all his many endearing qualities, Witty has the sort of face that seems made of spare parts, none of which were meant to go together. His nose hits you first. One of those extra large numbers that looks like it's been broken more than once. His eyes, which are washed out blue like faded Levis, are kind of small and close together, and when Witt gets upset they kind of seem to fuse into this one Cyclopean unit of blazing rage. He's got one of those Dudley DoRight chins, with the manly cleft and all, and a wide open forehead, perfect for smashing beer cans against. All in all, a face a mother could love, but many younger females have failed at the attempt. So, though I wasn't surprised to see Witty's eyes flare like a pair of tiny lighters at a rock concert when he got his first glimpse of Rosalie, I could only hope his misery would be short-lived.

I introduced them, anyway, since, technically, they would be teammates, even if Rosalie did nothing more than stand around in right field swatting gnats.

Rosalie smiled at Witt, and I could see it hit him hard. Then she said, "Eduardo said he would come also."

A ripple of doubt went through me as I remembered what Glory had said about Eduardo's crush on Rosalie. If Eduardo noticed the way Witty was gawking at Rosalie, it might throw him off his game. I was going to need all my diplomatic skills to keep everyone in the right frame of mind for the tournament. While Rosalie strolled to the outfield, I pulled Witty aside and explained the Eduardo scenario in a few well chosen words.

"Just tell me this," he said tersely. "Is she his girlfriend?"

"Well, no. Not officially."

"So he's got no claim on her?"

"Right. But, we need to keep him happy."

Witty shook his head stubbornly. "Why does he get to be happy? What about me being happy? You saw the way she looked at me. I've got a shot. She's the one. I can feel it. You can't expect me to sit back and let some cook move in on her."

"Listen, Witt, I'm just asking you to keep it low profile till after the tournament. Can't you do that for the team? For Glory? For me?"

He glared at the ground and pounded his glove moodily for a minute. Then he glanced toward the outfield. Rosalie waved and beamed at him sunnily. His mouth fell open, and he stared wordlessly for a moment. I don't know how long he might have stood there if Eduardo's car hadn't pulled up then and stopped with a loud backfire which, in retrospect, seemed almost Sophoclean in its portentousness. Hearing it, Witty turned to me and muttered, "I can't promise anything."

"Can you just try to keep it secret?"

Witty's gaze darted in Eduardo's direction. Eduardo was pulling a bat out of the backseat of his car. Seeing him outside the kitchen, and without his chef's jacket for the first time, I was struck by the size of his biceps, which bulged like Bridgestone tires from his sleeveless T-shirt. Witty watched thoughtfully as Eduardo started swinging the bat, loosening up his shoulders. Finally Witt turned back to me and said, "I'll keep it quiet till after the tournament."

"Great! That's all I ask." I breathed a sigh of relief and trotted out to have a few words with Darren on the mound while Witty put on a mask and got behind home plate. Luckily, Photon and Amanda showed up to help in the outfield, so we wouldn't have to waste too much time chasing balls. I moved into the shortstop position.

"Okay Darren, let's see what you got," I said.

Darren, who had been waving his arms windmill style for the last few minutes while he waited, pulled his arms close into his chest and stared toward the plate with a blank expression. Clouds floated silently across the high blue sky and locusts whirred like castanets in the still hot air while we waited for Darren to swing into action. He kept standing there motionless until finally I asked, "What are you waiting for?"

"Ain't he sposed to signal me? Tell me what kind a pitch he wants?"

I sighed. "Just throw the ball. We'll worry about signals later, okay?"

Darren shrugged. Then he lowered his chin till it met his glove, and he seemed to freeze for an instant, and I was just about to tell him to cut the crap because we didn't have all day, when his leg shot out in front of him as if he were trying to kick some invisible assassin in the face, and suddenly the ball flew towards the plate. Unfortunately, it hit the plate, bounced up and caught Eduardo on the knee, followed by a rain of Cuban invective.

"Sorry," muttered Darren. "Just warming up."

Eduardo tapped his bat against the plate. "Hokay. Try again," he said.

The next pitch flew out of Witty's reach, about six feet wide of the plate. Witty pulled up his mask so he could glare properly, first at Darren, then at me, before he trudged to the backstop to retrieve the ball. He tossed it back to Darren, who went into his petrified crane position again, and I was just starting to think maybe this wasn't such a hot idea when the ball whizzed toward the plate again, and suddenly Eduardo became a blur and there was a bang like a cherry bomb. The ball sailed high, deep and long, way beyond where Photon stood sneaking glances at Rosalie.

Eduardo grinned. Darren said, "Whoa." Then he looked at me and said, "You got any other balls?"

I gave him a look. "Yeah. We've got more balls. But let's try to make this one last, okay?" I saw that Rosalie had skipped into the high grass past the mowed outfield and was looking for the ball. I did have a bag of balls in the trunk of my car, but I couldn't afford to throw away balls, so I was glad to see her straighten up after a minute holding the ball above her head. When she attempted to toss it to Photon, it fell short into the tall grass again. I watched with a sinking feeling as she recovered the ball and tried again, without success, to throw it to Photon. I can't say I was surprised, but I guess I'd been hoping for miracles. A fantastic cook she might be. An incredibly hot babe she indisputably was. But, any hopes I might have had about Rosalie somehow contributing in any tangible way to the team more or less sank in the tall grass after I saw her throw.

Still, on the plus side, Eduardo delivered the goods, as Glory had promised he would. In the next hour, during which Darren's pitching remained erratic as the flight path of a fruit fly, Eduardo nonetheless managed to smack the ball repeatedly well beyond the outfield. If he could hit this well off someone as flakey as Darren, I felt confident that he would do well against the slow steady pitching of the Firemen, and even the tricky stuff Jenny hurls. She's got those curveballs and sliders and stuff. Kind of amazing for a girl. But that's Jenny.

Anyway, by the time we stopped Eduardo was glowing. Photon came in from the outfield chortling about how he couldn't wait to see the looks on the other teams' face when they got a load of Eduardo's hitting. I turned toward Witty and felt a sharp chill, as if someone had just emptied the water jug over my head even though we hadn't won the tournament yet. For there was Rosalie, shyly smiling at Witty. It was then I noticed that, despite my pleading, he was staring at her like an affectionate Labrador who wants to be taken for a walk. And she looked like she was open to the idea. I hustled over to Rosalie and suggested that we had better hurry back to the café, since the dinner shift would be underway soon, and Glory would be antsy. Rosalie said something in French that I didn't quite get, but she got in her car and left, and I turned to Witty to admonish him for not sticking to the script.

I caught him as he was getting into his truck. He held up his hand, stop sign style, as I tried to speak. "I know what you're gonna say and I don't care," he said. "You just don't understand love, Duggie. You never have. And I'm sorry, but I don't think you ever will. You can't fight love, Duggie. I've just found the love of my life, and I'm not going to let her go just because of some stupid softball game." He snorted as he started his engine. "Get a grip," he said, and backed off the field.

I have to say, as I watched him drive off, the effervescent mood I'd been enjoying ever since Eduardo's first hit dissipated rapidly as I considered Witty's words. I knew what he was like. A man of quick passions and rapid action. I wouldn't put it past him to go straight to the kitchen and propose to Rosalie without even bothering to go on a date with her first. It wouldn't be the first time for Witty.

Then I calmed down when I reflected that, even if he was as impulsive as a four-year-old, it was unlikely that Rosalie had developed a reciprocal level of insanity so early in the proceedings. I'm not saying it couldn't happen. Love is love, after all. As Terence noted, *amantes sunt amentes*—lovers are lunatics. I decided that the best thing I could do at this point was to consult Morris. If there was a way to slow down the rate at which all hell broke loose, Morris would know.

I could feel my heart rate slowing to a pleasant reggae beat even before I got up the mountain, and I don't think the joint I lit up as soon as I got out of town was totally responsible, although, of course, it helped. It always does. Opens the little windows in the mind and lets the breeze blow through. So what if Witty drools over Rosalie for the entire summer? Eduardo was a man of the world. And a hell of a ball player. Not to mention an amazing chef. His self-confidence might give him immunity to jealousy. He couldn't possibly see Witty as a threat. Not with that face. Witty's I mean.

By the time I stopped the truck I almost felt like I shouldn't bother Morris. It was late. But then I decided maybe he thought I was avoiding him because of our little disagreement over the pot bus, and I didn't want him to think that. Even though he was being shortsighted and paranoid about my plan, I could be big about it. He meant well.

So, I got out of the truck and was about ten feet from the door when a voice in the dark said, "Nice night." I nearly jumped out of my shorts. Then I realized the voice was familiar, and peering closer as my eyes adjusted to the mood lighting, I saw Morris sitting on one of the chairs outside my shack. I was glad to see him, not only because it meant I wouldn't have to walk up the path through the woods to his house, but, more importantly, because, I reasoned, maybe his being there meant he had thought about it and realized he had been wrong about the pot bus. Even though I know I'm right, I have to admit I've been a little nervous since the plants started booming. They're getting so huge, I'm beginning to think I might need some help when it comes time to bundle them.

Also, the fact that Morris had appeared right when I was about to go looking for him encouraged me to hope that things were okay between us. I mean, one of the things that makes Morris different from anyone else I know is the way he seems to be on some kind of parallel path with me. It's like, okay, we have different goals. He's a successful published novelist. I'm not. But I'm good at what I do, so that's success too, and after all, as the fellow said, *frustra laborat qui omnibus placere studet*—he labors in vain who tries to please everyone. I think Morris accepts me the way I am, for the most part.

"It's been a while," he said, in that quiet tone of voice like Lee Marvin before he pulls out the gun. It was then I noticed that he was smoking a joint, probably rolled from my own stash. Not that I mind. Morris knows he's always welcome to the refreshments at my house. But, it kind of irked me. Seems hypocritical, you know? First he tells me I shouldn't grow it, and then he comes over and smokes mine? I mean, come on.

I sat down and reached for the joint. He passed it to me and I took a deep toke and waited till the rush settled before I spoke. "Well, actually, I thought you were avoiding me."

"Why would I do that?"

I frowned. If Morris has a bad habit, it is that he sometimes falls into this Socratic mode where he answers every question with another question. Supposedly, this helps you to discover the truth. As if that would help.

"I thought you were still mad about the bus."

"I'm not mad." He blew a long plume of smoke into the air above his head. "I'll come visit you in prison."

"I'm not going to prison."

Morris didn't say anything. But it was the way he didn't that rankled. I decided to take the high road, hah, so to speak, and change the subject.

"Shitley's entering a team in the tournament."

"More the merrier."

I didn't feel particularly merry on this point myself, but I went on to explain the whole Jenny/Eduardo/Rosalie/Witt scenario, and when I finished I could tell by the lengthy pause that Morris appreciated the complexity of the equation.

"Sounds like you'll have your hands full," he said finally, and, though I couldn't see his face in the dark, I could tell he was more amused than concerned.

"Actually, I was going to ask if you had any ideas for how to get through this."

"You'll get through it."

"I know that. It's not me I'm worried about. Glory's really counting on winning the tournament to keep Eduardo from being seduced by Shitley's riches."

"Shitley wants to seduce Eduardo?"

I frowned. When Morris gets stoned his Socratic cross-talk routine gets even more annoying.

"Shitley wants to hire Eduardo because he's heard how good he is, and he's afraid Glory's going to get another star."

Morris was quiet for a few moments, and I hoped he was analyzing the various aspects of the impending disaster with an eye toward heading it off.

Several more minutes drifted over the horizon before he spoke, and I confess my mind had wandered to speculation about whom Jenny would be recruiting for the Swans. A bubble of optimism rose as I considered that, even though Jenny and Babe were a formidable unit, without some other half decent players on their team they wouldn't pose much of a threat to the Moonlighters.

"Rosalie is the key to your problem."

I shook myself. "How do you mean?"

"Find out what Rosalie wants, and promise it to her in exchange for her cooperation. She's the linchpin. If you get her to work with you, she can manage Witt and keep Eduardo on a leash until after the tournament at least."

"Well, duh. I know that. But what if she doesn't want to—"

"Play ball?"

"Yeah. What then?"

"You know, for a hippie child of god you worry more than you should."

"Thanks. I'll work on it."

"Of course, I'd be worried too if I had a busload of felonious contraband in my backyard."

"It'll be gone soon."

"Won't we all?"

"Thanks for the support. I feel so much better now."

"You don't think it's the pot talking?"

"I was being ironic."

"Ah. Irony."

"What's that supposed to mean?"

"What do you think?"

"Cut that out."

"Cut what out?"

"You know what I mean."

"You think so?"

I got up and went inside. When he gets like this you just have to wait for it to run its course.

Morris seemed to vanish after that, so I got into bed and was almost asleep when the phone rang. I considered not answering, but the noise was so shrill I gave in and picked up.

"Duggie?"

"Who else would it be?" Morris does this to me. Revives the little Plato napping in my subconscious.

"Are you all right? I didn't think you'd be in bed already."

Sitting up groggily I realized this wasn't Morris after all. Morris would never apologize for waking me since he thinks I spend too much time slacking off as it is. No. It was Eric, the most polite, self-effacing guy I know.

"It's okay. What's up?" I asked. There was a moment of silence. "Eric? You still there?"

"Yeah. Listen, Duggie, I hate to do this, but I wanted to let you know as soon as possible because I don't want to let you down, but . . . the thing is . . . well, that's why I'm calling."

"What do you mean?" I said, feeling suddenly wide awake and apprehensive.

"Well, it's like this. You know how I'm trying to get Amanda to go out with me?"

"Right."

"And now that Jenny's putting together a team for the Black Swan, she's been asking around. You know, recruiting?"

I could see this coming like a pie in the face.

"So, I asked her if I could be on her team."

"Wait! Let me get this straight. She didn't come to you? You went to her and *asked* to be on her team?"

"That's right. See, Amanda told me that she's going to play for Jenny, and so I thought it would help if we were on the same team. You know? Practicing together, playing together. She'll see me as a guy, not just a customer."

"And you think that'll help?" I didn't want to burst his balloon, but seriously, though Eric is my friend and there's nobody I'd rather have on my team if I'm playing Trivial Pursuit or Simpsons' Jeopardy, when it comes to softball, Eric's not exactly A-team material. He understands the rules as well as anyone, but he's got a classic nerd physique with the athletic ability to match. So, losing him to Jenny, not such a blow. Naturally I had to pretend I was upset.

"Jeez man. I can't believe you're deserting me for a girl."

"Hey. You don't need me. You've got Witt, and the chef guy. I hear he's hot stuff."

"You mean Eduardo? Yeah. He's pretty good." I didn't let on about Eduardo. If Eric were still on the Moonlighters I would have been upfront, but, since he'd gone to the competition, I figured no sense tipping our hand. Better to let the other teams think they have a chance so they don't start recruiting ringers.

"Seriously, Duggie. You guys'll be fine without me. And I really think this could give me a chance with Amanda. She sounded really pleased when I told her I was going to join the team."

"Really?"

"Yeah. Turns out, have you heard? Her ex-boyfriend, DK? He's put together a team of his lowlife jock friends. They've been playing in some dirtball league in Prince William. Amanda says she heard from one of her girlfriends who used to date one of the players that DK is already bragging about how he's going to come to Rapidan and kick some ass."

"Really?"

"Yeah. So, it's a good opportunity for me to stand up to him and impress Amanda."

The enthusiasm in Eric's voice was almost painful to hear. The guy was so far out of touch with reality he would need a passport to approach normal. But, of course, I didn't point this out. I just said, "Well, great. Good luck with that."

I hung up thinking he would need a lot more than mere luck. And then it hit me, like a coconut falling from the tree. With Amanda and Eric both defecting, we were now short three players, and I had no idea where to dredge up replacements. Add to this the news that DK was planning to ride rough over the tournament, and it would have taken a better man than I to laugh it off. I lay down in darkness and mused on the ominous specter of Doyle Krump looming like a thunderhead.

Chapter 4

Qui me amat, amat et canem meam.
He who loves me loves my dog.

The rich aroma of warm dog breath on my face ushered in the new day. I opened my eyes with a mild sense of surprise that they had shut last night after what had seemed like an eternity of scurrying through the back pages of my mind trying to hit upon a plan to thwart Doyle Krump and his horde.

And, despite the fact that a quick review of the evidence showed that I had, as yet, failed to find the magic ring or secret plan which would enable me to dismantle this new threat to the Moonlighters, I was feeling great. Rufie thwapped his tail happily against my leg, clearly hoping that we would go for a run. I glanced at the clock Glory gave me to ensure my timely arrival at work. I hated to disappoint Rufie again. This whole employment situation was seriously cutting into my real life.

"Okay, pal. Glory's gonna be pissed, but we'll do one lap around the perimeter, okay?"

Rufie started bouncing on his front legs, raring to go, as usual. It's a good thing I'm not one of those people who keeps a bunch of knick knacks and mementoes covering all the tables and what not, not that I have much furniture to begin with. If I did, Rufie would have made short work of it. He's not a huge dog, but his general gung ho attitude makes him seem considerably larger than he is.

As soon as I finished tying on my trainers we burst out the front door and nearly collided with Amanda. She was huddled in my favorite chair, the metal one that rocks when you do, and she was vibrating like an unbalanced tea kettle about to blow.

She raised her face to look at me, and I was shocked to see it was all pink and shiny with tears. It seemed awfully early in the morning for that sort of thing, even for a girl, so I called Rufie back—he was already bounding up the trail.

"Glory fired me," she squeaked.

"What for?"

"We were talking about the tournament, and she said something about Jenny quitting the Moonlighters, so I thought it would be a good time to tell her."

"Tell her what?"

"That I'm going to play for Jenny. She's my sister. She asked me. And you know I'm not any good. But Jenny doesn't want to play against me, and I don't want to play against her. So . . ."

I nodded. I hadn't given a thought to Amanda not being on the team, to tell the truth, because, no offense to all womankind, but, really, when they were passing out athletic skills in the Carson family they lumped it all on Jenny. Amanda is one of those arty, sensitive type girls who don't get sports at all. So, I had been almost relieved when Eric told me she was going to play for Jenny. But I could see she was upset about losing her job.

"I can't believe she fired you because of the tournament. You don't think there was any other reason?"

Amanda sniffed and felt in her pocket for a tissue. She blew her nose, and said, "Well. I know I'm not a very good waitress. But, I'm just in the stupid diner. It's not like it's a big deal."

I studied her face for a moment. Although she doesn't have that dark hair and those dark eyes like her sister, she does have a certain pixie quality. I could understand why Eric was smitten. "Listen," I said, "whenever I get fired from a job, I always look at it as an opportunity. You've got to figure it's part of the Big Plan, and that better things are in store for you. Especially you. You should be running an art gallery or something."

"Thanks. I knew you would cheer me up," she said. Then she balled up the tissue and sighed. "The trouble is, there's nothing out here, you know? I can't just keep mooching off Jenny. I don't want to have to move into the city. But there's no jobs out here. At least in the city I could find work."

I frowned. If Amanda moved back into D.C., it would be bad for Eric. He's tried to cut it in the city before and failed. He's basically not hard-nosed enough, or slick enough, or pushy enough. That's why he belongs out here in Rapidan where nice guys don't finish last because nobody cares about finishing so much. We're all about the process. The journey. All that Buddhist stuff. Anyway. I looked at Amanda and thought there must be some way I could fix this. I mean, she came to me for help. And Eric would want me to help. So maybe Fate expected me to come up with something.

We sat there listening to the mourning doves doing that thing they do for a few minutes, and then a slippery little idea came to me like a skink slithering past a sleeping cat.

"What are your feelings about breaking the law?" I asked.

She looked at me and cocked her head to one side. "I guess it depends on the law."

"Let's say it's one of those unnecessary intrusive kind of laws that just creates busy work for cops in low crime areas."

Amanda raised her eyebrows. "I suppose if that's the case, then I'm flexible."

"So, you agree that marijuana should be legal?"

"Isn't it?"

I smiled. I could see the way clear ahead like a freeway of love. "Not around here, but it should be. The reason I'm asking is, I don't think you should move back to the city just to get some crappy job when you can get a crappy job out here."

"Do you have some crappy job in mind?"

"Well, yes. It occurs to me that I might be in need of an assistant for a project I have underway. But, it's a sort of undercover project. So I can't tell you what it is unless you can agree to maintain secrecy and silence."

Amanda smiled, and the resemblance to Jenny shot up by a thousand degrees. "I can't promise until I know what it is."

"Okay. But you have to promise not to tell anyone, even if you decide not to do it, okay?"

She shrugged. "Okay. I promise not to tell anyone. Whatever."

I glanced around to make sure no one had slinked through the woods while we were talking, even though I knew that Rufie would have given them the big doggie howl hello before they got close. But sometimes he forgets, like when Jenny comes with a bag of dog biscuits. As soon as I was sure we were alone, I told Amanda about the pot bus, and how I could use some help getting the plants to the finished stage. In the beginning, when they were small, it was easy to schlep jugs of fertilizer into the bus. But now, it was getting more complicated. And once they start blooming it will be another job to cut and dry the plants. A lot of work.

Amanda quickly grasped the essentials and agreed to come in on the project for a share of the proceeds. Also, I added dog exerciser to her job description because it occurred to me that Rufie would be pleased to be taken for a run more often, and then, when I get home from the restaurant, and I want to sit quietly and do nothing, Rufie will already be worn out and ready to do nothing with me. It's one of our best things.

As I drove down to the café a short while later I was feeling fairly well pleased with this new solution to two, no three, little problems that had developed. I had help with the bus crop. Rufie had a new exercise program. And Amanda had a new job, working for a more evolved employer, which meant she wouldn't be leaving Eric to mope around like the lovesick English major that he is. All in all a good morning's work, and I hadn't even gotten to my so-called job.

As it turned out, it was a good thing I was in such a mellow mood when I arrived, because Glory was in rare ass-kicking form. I could hear her voice from the parking lot outside the kitchen, and it made me feel even better about having rescued Amanda from the fire-breathing dragon that is my sister when she's not happy.

"Oh, it's you," she said, as I tried to slip in quietly.

I flashed the sunny smile, which sometimes does the trick. Not today.

"Nice of you to show up, since we have twenty customers arriving in less than an hour and somebody forgot to start the dishwasher before he went home last night so they're going to have to be done by hand right now." She glared at me in a pointed way, and I felt a quiver of memory. Had I forgotten to push the button on the big machine last night? Possibly. I had a lot on my mind at the time. But, no problem. I gave Glory another reassuring smile and said, "No problem. I'm on it."

"That is the problem," she snapped. I ignored the taunt and plunged into work with the soapy water.

As usual, by the time the lunch shift was winding down and the waiters were comparing tips, Glory's wrath had abated. I could tell by the way she punched my shoulder when she went past as I was loading the dishwasher.

"So, what'd you think of Eduardo?" she asked.

"He's great. I just hope he can hit that well off a real pitcher."

Glory frowned. "What do you mean? Who've we got now?"

I filled her in quickly on the Darren situation, and I could see it didn't sit well with her. "You shouldn't blame Jenny," I said. "She'd rather play for us, I know."

"It's not her I blame. It's that bastard Shitley. He's going to muck up the whole tournament."

"I don't think it will be as bad as that."

"Oh no? Did you hear he's bought hats? And shirts?"

"Really? Are you going to get us hats?"

"No! That's what I'm talking about. Have we ever had hats? Has anybody ever had uniforms, for God's sake? What does he think this is? The World Series?"

I pretended to be absorbed in arranging the dishes for maximum efficiency, but I couldn't deny the pang of envy that pinched me at the thought of the Swans swanking around in matching hats and shirts. After a moment I said, "You know, maybe it would be cool for us to have hats? You know? You could sell Moonlighters hats here for customers."

Glory folded her arms and glared at me the way she used to when we were kids and I questioned her interpretation of the Monopoly rules. "I am not selling tacky hats here."

"They wouldn't have to be tacky. They could be tasteful, understated. I bet Amanda could make a nice logo." I stopped. I had gone too far. Glory's expression hardened into her patented Boardwalk Brush-off.

"Don't talk to me about Amanda," she snarled.

"You shouldn't hold it against her."

"Why not?"

"Well, for one thing, she's a lousy ball player. She'll be helping us more by playing on their team."

Glory's frown lines shortened. "Hmm. Something in that, I guess. Still. It's the principal of the thing."

"It's just softball," I said, even though I didn't believe it for a minute. It was only the most important social event of the year. Which is why hats would be so great. But when you're negotiating with short-tempered employers who happen to be related to you by blood ties, there are times when a little gray half-truth is your best line of attack.

Glory gave a Marge Simpson style grunt and walked away. I had finished my post lunch chores, so I went out the back door and headed for a bench under a humongous willow tree by the creek that flows behind the restaurant. I had a nice skinny reefer in my pocket and a few hours to kill before the dinner shift kicked in. I was planning to give some thought to the new vacancies on the team, now that Eric and Amanda were off the roster.

I was almost out of sight of the restaurant when I heard a panting noise behind me. Before I could turn around a hard shove in the back nearly knocked me to the grass. "Hey!" I yelled. I turned and saw Jenny, but the smile on my face wilted when I saw the cold fury in her eyes.

"Are you totally, completely insane?" she began. "What's the big idea getting my sister involved in your criminal schemes? Doesn't she have enough problems?"

I hesitated. I confess, it hadn't occurred to me that Jenny might not exactly approve of Amanda helping out with the pot bus. But of course, now that I thought about it, I could see how, from a purely conventional point of view, it might not seem the best of plans.

"There's nothing to worry about," I began.

"You freaking idiot! How about getting busted? How about getting sent to prison? How about having your future career completely screwed because some moron talked you into watering his pot crop?" She shook her head and stared at me with a level of scorn that would have done Glory proud. Not pleasant, but at least I wasn't stoned so I wasn't afraid she was going to hit me, although she looked like the idea may have crossed her mind.

"Listen, if it bothers you so much, forget it. I'll tell her I changed my mind."

Jenny snorted. "She won't believe that."

"Why not?"

"Because she knows you're kind of helpless. And now she's all excited about making a pile of money. She's even looking forward to walking your dog! If I didn't know any better I'd think she was on something. She came home this morning all bubbling about how she was going to be a slacker entrepreneur like you."

I wobbled at this. The term was new to me. "A slacker entrepreneur?"

Jenny shrugged. "She says it's like the dot-com millionaires except more under the radar. I don't know what she's talking about. Apparently she's always admired the way you manage to get by without working a real job. The way you just lurk around like a slug, getting stoned and playing cards and never having any responsibility. Now she thinks she can do it too. So help me Duggie, if you ruin her life I'll kill you."

I stared at her. Like a slug, I suppose, if slugs stare. Hard to tell if they have eyes, now that I think of it. I didn't know what to say, but I took a stab at it. I'd never seen Jenny so mad at me.

"Listen, I'm sorry. I was just trying to help. She was crying and I thought it would give her something to do . . . you know . . . keep her mind off Krump and stuff."

"She doesn't care about Krump."

"Really? That's great."

Jenny stood there grinding her teeth, pounding her fist against her thigh. I was having a hard time concentrating on the immediate issue. "So . . . are we okay then?" I asked.

"No! How could we be okay? I can't force her not to work for you, and you're too spineless to talk her out of it." She fumed for a moment, swatting at the gnats swirling above us. "How much longer until you're through with the bus?" she said.

"I don't know. They're coming along really fast because of the lights I think. It might be just another couple of weeks. Maybe less."

"So then, what? You cut it, wrap it and get rid of it?"

"Right."

Jenny sighed heavily and frowned at the grass. "I guess there's nothing we can do but hope one of your sleazy buddies doesn't blow your cover."

"Nobody knows. Except you. And Eric. And now Amanda. And Morris. But, that's all. Nobody else knows."

"How about the guy you're selling it to?"

"Well, yeah. Him. But he doesn't know where I live. I've got it all worked out. And I won't let Amanda be anywhere around when the deal goes down. If I'm gonna get busted, which I'm not, that would be when it would happen."

Jenny shook her head and looked at me as if I were a puppy she was housetraining who hadn't quite made it to the paper again. "You'd better be right."

"Trust me. I know what I'm doing."

"Pah. You don't even know enough not to say that. It's amazing you haven't been locked up before this."

She turned and walked back toward the restaurant. I watched her walk, wishing there were something I could say that would make her laugh. But at the moment it didn't seem likely. When she disappeared from view, I turned and finished walking to the bench.

I lit up the joint and inhaled deeply and felt an immediate improvement in my outlook. So Jenny was worried. Perfectly natural. She'd calm down once it was all over. I bet she'd even laugh about it. With me. I could picture us together, laughing.

There I was, staring at the stream, lost in thought as usual, and, at first I thought maybe it was my imagination adding special effects, but I could have sworn I heard laughter floating on the breeze. I sat up and looked around. The sound appeared to be real and coming from the Black Swan's parking lot. The Swan backs onto this same stream, and has a kind of terrace with tables that overlook the water.

For some reason, the laughter struck me as sinister, and I don't know why, but I felt an irresistible urge to go and investigate. I made my way across the grassy space and crept under the cover of a weeping tree of some kind that grew beside the Swan's roadside parking area. I could hear voices, so boisterous and clear that I flinched for fear of being seen. Shipley was standing in the sun, talking to some dressed-up woman. She looked like a TV reporter. She had that plastic Stepford Wife sheen you never see on women in Rapidan. Shipley was giving her the high test oil, you could tell by the phony shine in his eyes, clearly visible from my hidden vantage point.

"You should come back on the Fourth of July and see our little tournament," he said, smiling like a real estate agent.

"Oh really? What sort of tournament? Horseshoes?" The woman simpered—one of those professional simpers that's even worse than the real thing.

"No. It's softball. Good old American game. Family fare. We have a team from the restaurant. A few of the other locals play. It's a good community building tradition. Your readers might like to hear about it."

"Maybe so. Perhaps we can send a photographer at least. I'll talk to my editor."

They chuckled some more and lowered their voices so I missed the last bit, but I'd heard enough. Damn Shipley. We don't need news coverage.

However, as I continued to lurk under the tree, brooding on this new development, another thought squeezed to the front of the crowd and started tugging on my cloaking device. The Moonlighters were still short-handed, and I couldn't think of anyone left to recruit, unless we put a shirt on Rufie. A hat probably wouldn't stay on anyway.

I decided to stroll down to the bowling alley in the hope of finding inspiration there. The sun was beginning to singe the grass growing in the cracks of the asphalt, and I was feeling a bit wilted on by the time I covered the four blocks to the Strike Zone. The door howled like a hungry primate as I pushed through into the dank twilight. The neon Budweiser sign, missing its "d," cast a siren coral glow along the bar. The place was practically empty, as you would expect on a sunny weekday midafternoon. I took a seat on one of the stools and peered into the shadows, looking for any sign of life. A shape slumping against the back of one of the booths along the wall shifted, and I caught a glimpse of coral. I squinted into the darkness.

"Kevin? Is that you?"

"Got it in one, Duggie." The braces on his smile glittered with reflected bar light.

"What are you doin' in here?" I asked. "I thought you got sent up to JuVee camp."

The glitter vanished. "I got that straightened out. The old man cut me some slack."

"Hmmph. I guess you ought to get some perks for being the Sheriff's son."

"That's what I said."

"And he agreed?" Never having been on what you might call cozy terms with this Sheriff Ed Quayle, I found it hard to believe that the man had a compassionate bone in his body, even if you counted his head, which was more or less solid bone. But, again, I digress.

"You working here now? Or just for the summer?"

"Just for the summer. Or until I get on my Dad's good side again." He smiled again, like a ferret enjoying a private joke.

"Yeah. Well. Good luck with that," I said and slid off the bar stool to leave, not being a great fan of Kevin Quayle's idea of repartee, which tends to draw heavily from Howard Stern. But, before I got to the door, it hit me. Sure, he was a repulsive little reptile and about as trustworthy as a copperhead, but he could probably run. And presumably he understood the rudiments of softball. And, I was feeling a little desperate. I turned back to him. He was staring at me. His eyes looked like a pair of little black marbles trying to roll into each other across the bridge of his sharp nose.

"I need a few more players for the team, for the tournament. You interested?"

His face lit up like a highway flare. "You want me to be on the Moonlighters?"

"Can you do it?"

Kevin's grin slipped a little sideways as he nodded his head. "Oh yeah. That would be real good. I'd be glad to . . . help you out." He kind of smirked as he said this, and I fought the impulse to withdraw the offer. But then I thought, what if someone else gets hurt or can't play for some other reason? As it was, even with Kevin, I still had to find one more player. I couldn't afford to be choosy. As the fellow said, *ad praesens ova cras pullis sunt meliora*. Eggs today are better than chickens tomorrow. Even a rotten egg.

CHAPTER 5

Nemo mortalium omnibus horis sapit.
No mortal is wise at all times.
Pliny the Elder

A lesser man might have wasted valuable time worrying during the week that followed. But I take a line from Virgil: *cur ante tubam tremor occupat artus?* Why should fear seize the limbs before the trumpet sounds? Which is just a fancy way of saying worry is pointless. Action is the key. Some people get confused, thinking that the action has to be related to the subject of the worry. This is a common misconception. I have found, through years of field research in stress avoidance and time management, that the best way to deal with worry is to order it to its room with no supper while you, meanwhile, go out to a party, or, failing that, a bar, or, if neither of these is an option, a bracing game of cards with a group of congenial souls. This might not sound productive to those of you who insist on linear thinking, but let me assure you that solutions are shy slippery things which must be tricked into showing themselves. If they think you're looking for them, they can hole up for days, weeks even. But if they see you yukking it up with the boys, careless and merry, they begin to feel insecure and out of sorts. All solutions exist to be needed. If they think you might learn to do without them, they pop up like worms after a soaking rain.

So my first strategic move was to send out the word that Hearts would be dealt on the porch at Morris's on Saturday night. I didn't bother to ask Morris if this would be okay, because Morris is a student of human nature. And, although he rarely plays, he sometimes weighs in with a *bon mot* or two. I always bring extra reefer for him. He never turns it down.

Still, I was surprised on Saturday as I emerged from the woods on the path to Morris's to see a lithe young nymph tripping lightly down the stairs from his porch. I couldn't see her face before she slipped into her car, but I caught a snatch of her voice as she warbled goodbye. By the time I reached the edge of the drive the dust she had kicked up on the road was drifting back into place.

"Who was that?" I asked Morris as I got within hailing range.

"Why do you want to know?"

I paused. Evasive replies are Morris's stock in trade, but I was still surprised. It's not as if he ever has women at his place. I mean, never. He could be one of those monks under a vow of celibacy except for the divorced past. Anyway. The point is, you don't see women at Morris's. I've tried to probe him on the subject before, but he gets cryptic and annoying, so I gave it up.

"Come on, man. Who was that? Your long lost daughter? A desperate grad student?"

Morris raised his eyebrows. "She's one of your friends."

I sank into a chair on the porch and commenced rocking. "Who?"

"You didn't recognize her?"

"I didn't get a good enough look." Sunlight was fast fading from the sky, I should mention. A sprinkling of fireflies capered in the tall grass.

Morris lit a cigarette. Disgusting habit. I've told him to quit. He always counters with tiresome 'facts' about marijuana lowering your IQ.

He blew out a long trail of smoke. He claims he does it to discourage the mosquitoes. I think the mosquitoes are addicted to nicotine.

"Her name is Phoebe. She was here about the cats."

I reeled. "You have cats?"

"I don't have cats. A cat moved in under the porch a few weeks ago and I couldn't convince it to leave."

"What methods did you try?"

"I didn't feed it."

Not good enough, I felt. Cats are notoriously self-sufficient. If you want a cat to leave, you have to create an environment that will convince the feline that staying is not in his or her best interests. Merely withholding the chow won't do. You start with pans of cold water, dumped from above, and work up to blasts from the hose, delivered with conviction and regularity. I didn't say this, of course. No one likes a know-it-all.

"Was it Phoebe's cat, then?"

"No. When I called the shelter, she answered the phone. She works there."

"Ah. So she cleared up the problem?"

"She took the cats."

"Plural?"

"The cat had kittens while it was under my porch."

"Ahah. Well, I'm glad you got it all cleared up before the game. It would have been a distraction having a pile of kittens meowing under the floorboards."

Morris gave me a look. It was more crammed with subtexts than a lit major's thesis, but I refused to get sucked into the trap. When Morris looks at me like that, it's his opening gambit in the chess mindgame. Pawn to what for. Instead, I pulled out a joint from my pocket and lit it up. Morris stubbed out his cigarette and reached for the joint. We didn't speak for the next couple of minutes. Concentrating on regular and deep inhaling, as not practiced by former President Bill Clinton if you believe that, my mind began wandering, and it came upon a fragment from Morris's earlier remarks.

"She said she knew me?"

"Who?"

"This cat girl."

"Phoebe?"

"If that's her name."

"You don't know her?"

"I don't think so. I could be wrong. You know. You meet someone at a party, you forget." I paused to cough. "What's she look like?"

"Perky. Blonde."

"Well, that narrows it down."

Morris shrugged. "Does it matter?"

"I thought I knew every girl in the county. I guess I missed one."

"You'll get another chance to see her tomorrow."

"She coming to the game?"

"She's going to be in the parade."

"Really? Normally I give that a miss. In what capacity will she be parading?"

"The shelter has a float. She'll be on it. With a cat on a leash."

"I didn't know you could put leashes on cats."

"I never said I could. Thankfully, since I have no cat, the need has never risen."

I looked at him. It was pretty dark on the porch by this time, and I could barely make out his expression, but I didn't have to see it to know he was just getting warmed up. "Never mind," I said. A few minutes later Witt drove up with Randall, his neighbor, who is a redneck but smokes weed anyway and is an all right guy. I sometimes think the redneck thing is a pose that he uses to get chicks, which doesn't make sense to me, but it works for him, so you can't argue with success.

"Duggieeee. How's ma boy?" Randall clapped me on the back, launching another volley of coughing. When it let up, I said hello and asked how his plumbing gig was going. Unlike the rest of us, Randall never wasted his youth in college classrooms learning arcane bits of useless information. He went straight to work right out of high school and got a grip on pipe wrenches and copper fittings and what not and has been making steady money ever since. Everyone needs a plumber sooner or later.

Randall also is a reliable second baseman, one of the most competent players on our team, especially now that Jenny is gone. I filled him in with the latest developments re Shitley and the Sandblasters. He took it better than I expected.

"So what? Shitley's a fathead and Krump's a tool, but we already knew that, right? So nothing's changed. We just gotta go out there and kick their butts good and proper." He smiled widely and blew a stream of smoke into my face.

"You're right. But, it could get ugly this year."

"Huh. With Krump and Shitley in the game, no way it can be anything but." Randall continued to beam. "Hey, if we still need another player, I can ask Gary. I think he played in high school."

"Ask him. Offer him money if need be," I said.

"You didn't offer me money," said Randall.

"You can have a finder's fee if you bring this guy on board. I just want to have a full team when we take the field tomorrow."

The screen door banged as Eric entered the porch. We all looked at him, and maybe it was the pot talking, but I had this weird heebiejeebie feeling, because he wasn't on our team for the first time ever.

He sat down and smiled in that shy spaniel way of his, and I realized it didn't matter. Eric's the kind of guy who plays the game, but he never saves the day. So you don't count on him to do it. Which is fine. We can't all be heroes. And, to his credit, he has never, to my knowledge, made a game-losing error either. So, pretty much a wash. Not like DK, who is evil to the core. Or Shitley, who is just plain offensive.

"Hey, Morris," said Eric, twisting the cap off a beer as I dealt the first hand. "Amanda told me her friend Phoebe helped you out."

"That's right."

Eric nodded. "I didn't know you had cats."

"I don't."

"But you did?"

"I never had cats."

I could see confusion spreading like a blush across Eric's face. I shot a look at Morris. "Some cats tried to move in with Morris. He lacked the skills to convince them to leave. This Phoebe resolved the crisis. A girl with advanced cat skills, she not only removed the original cat, but also a litter of bonus kittens."

"Really?"

"Really. And I don't think Morris even tipped her."

Eric looked quizzically at Morris, who shook his head and said, "Don't listen to him."

"You did tip her?"

"No."

"Oh." Eric puzzled over his cards for a moment before he spoke again. "Phoebe wouldn't care about a tip. She's all about karma."

"Oh god," scoffed Randall.

"There's nothing wrong with that," said Eric, frowning slightly.

"Pheh." Randall shook his head. "Sure. There's nothing wrong with it. Or with astrology or fung shu or any of that crap. She wants to believe in crystals, it's okay by me."

"Okay. She's kind of an airhead. But, she's really good with animals."

Randall shrugged and passed three cards to his left. For a minute we all concentrated on the subtleties of the pass, one of the finer points of the game. Once Witt put down the first card, a two of clubs for those of you playing along at home, conversation resumed.

"Speaking of animals, is it true that you told Kevin he could play on our team?" Witt fixed a steely gaze on me, and I felt a moment of doubt. I quickly rose above it.

"Yes. It's true."

"What were you thinking?"

I paused to select a heart to drop on the pile before responding. "I was thinking it would be better to have a full team than to play a man down."

"What, you don't have any clubs? And Kevin was the only option?"

I frowned. "No. But I ran into him and I took it as a sign."

"Duggie? I run into people all the time. I don't take it as a sign that I'm supposed to invite them into my life."

I could have said something fairly terse at this point, touching on a certain person's tendency to invite women to become soulmates after a mere glimpse in the grocery store, but I refrained. No point in stirring ire.

"Think of it as community service," I said.

"What, for him?"

"No, for us. We'll be helping him to become a better person by allowing him to participate in a wholesome activity."

"You're nuts," said Randall. "That kid's a creep and a lying son of a bitch. I wouldn't trust him to wash my dog."

"You could trust Phoebe," said Eric.

"Who?"

"Phoebe. The cat girl?"

"The karma chick?"

"Right." Eric scooped up the rest of the pile, and we counted cards for a minute in silence.

"I'm just saying," Witt resumed after he came back to the table with another beer, "it's bad for the team to have a creep like Quayle. We'd be better off playing a man down."

"Well, it's too late. I'm not going to kick him off the team. Besides, maybe he'll annoy the Sandblasters with his chatter."

"He's gonna annoy me," Witt grumbled.

Eric shifted in his chair and threw down the ten of spades. "From what Amanda has told me about Krump's team, I doubt they'll even notice he's alive."

We all turned to him. "What'd she tell you?" I asked.

"She says DK has been recruiting players from this team in Prince William that had some guys who tried out for the Cannons."

"So they tried out," said Witt. "But did they make the team?"

Eric lowered his chin and looked over his cards at Witt with an expression I would have to say was condescending, and that's rare for Eric unless the subject under discussion is 18th century romantic poets. "The point is, these are guys who are good enough to try out for the Cannons. Who on your team could do that?"

I shot a warning glance at Witt to stop him from bringing up Eduardo, but I needn't have worried. Despite the blank look in his eyes, I could tell by the way his jaw was clenched that Witt was already wearing his game face. He shrugged and said, "Huh. Guess they must think they're hot stuff."

The Cannons, in case you don't know, are a kind of minor league bunch who supposedly make a living playing baseball. No one's ever heard of them outside Virginia. Still, it seems only reasonable to assume that anyone who can fake it at that level is a few notches higher up on the sports evolutionary scale than the average Rapidan duffer. The mood darkened along with the night as we played on. It's a testament to how distracted we were that Randall was able to shoot the moon, a thing he never does.

"Well, there's a sign for you," said Witty, throwing his cards down in disgust.

"What do you mean?" said Randall. "I just got lucky."

"Don't kid yourself. We helped," Witty muttered, standing up. He stretched and let out a howl that jerked Rufie from the dreamless and drew an oath from Morris, who had been gazing quietly out at the stars.

"Do you mind not doing that?" he said.

"I'm through," said Witt. "I'm going."

I glanced at the clock through the window and suddenly had an uneasy premonition. "It's still early. Stay awhile."

"Nah. I got things to do."

I frowned. Knowing that Rosalie would be finished at the restaurant about this time, I could put two and two together as well as the next man, and better than some. I would have been willing to bet money, if I'd had any, that Witty was leaving for some mushy rendezvous. Ordinarily, I wouldn't care. But with the first game of the tournament tomorrow it was absolutely essential that nothing happened to unsettle Eduardo. These hitters are like thoroughbreds. If they get spooked it can throw them off their whole game.

I followed Witt out into the night and grabbed him by the elbow as he was opening the door of his truck. "Where are you going?" I asked, not beating around the bush.

"None of your business."

"Oh I think it is my business," I said, tightening my grip.

He yanked his elbow loose and spared me a baleful look. "Just back off, Duggie. I'm not Eric. I'm not asking you for advice. A man's gotta do what a man's gotta do." Saying this, he jumped in the cab of the truck and slammed the door. As the engine roared to life I pounded on the door and yelled through the window, "Try to be discreet!"

I don't know if he heard me.

When I trudged back to the porch I found Randall standing there waiting for me. "Can you give me a ride home, Duggie? Witt said he didn't think you'd mind."

Well, I couldn't say no, could I? Eric had already left, dashing off, no doubt, to see his new girlfriend. I could have been bitter, I suppose, but it's not my style. After all, if I didn't have my heart set on Jenny, I could have had a girlfriend. Possibly someone like this Phoebe chick, who apparently had fond memories of our meeting, though her name still drew a blank for me. So we bade a cheery goodnight to Morris, after splitting one farewell reefer with him, and then went back to my house. Randall was in a good mood, having been the big winner at the table. Normally I enjoyed Randall's breezy pseudo-redneck banter, but this night I was distracted by fears of *fama clamosa*. If word gets out of Witt's clandestine meeting with Rosalie, the effect on Eduardo would be like one of those tropical depressions that works up a head of mayhem while soaking up the thermals above the tropic sea. More rational men than Eduardo have been known to use baseball bats for purposes other than athletic competition.

After I dropped Randall off at the picturesque bungalow he shares with his current girlfriend Marlene, I drove home in a somber mood. But, as often happens, once I was alone with Rufie, with the windows down and the night air wafting through my hair,

I began to calm down. Rufie had his head out the shotgun window, enjoying the scent of honeysuckle and the rustle of wildlife. It was a warm night, with a bit of moon adding silvery shadows to the scene. My inner tranquility had just about returned to its happy place when I turned off the engine and got out of the car. I stood there for a moment drinking in the peace.

And then, there was this flicker of something. Like when the electricity blinks just before it goes out for eight hours. I felt a shudder of unease. I froze, and in the darkness, which of course suddenly seemed a lot darker than it had just a moment before, moonglow notwithstanding, I thought I could detect a gentle murmur, as if a couple of fairies or elves or other forest types had gathered around the watercooler and were discussing last night's Daily Show.

I concentrated my powers of detection and realized with a chilling dread that the noise was coming from the direction of the bus. My heart started thumping so hard I worried that it might be audible to whoever or whatever was nearby. I crouched lower and began creeping toward the bus, taking care not to snap any twigs.

Unfortunately, I had failed to take into account Rufie's unbounded enthusiasm for adventure. He sprang ahead into the underbrush with a racket that sounded like a string of firecrackers exploding. The small ones. But still. Not anything like stealthy.

Figuring my cover was blown, I swallowed my fear and stood up, ready to face whatever fate had in store. And I'll be darned, but my courage was instantly rewarded by the sound of musical laughter. Girlish musical laughter, the best kind. I picked up speed and quickly closed the distance on the bus, and there, by the golden plant light spilling from the bus's open door, I saw Amanda and Eric making out.

Well, you can imagine my relief, but, almost instantly it was accompanied by a cold shower of petulance. I mean, if these two lovebirds want to sing a duet they should do it on their own turf is my feeling, and I said so.

Eric startled at the sound of my voice and banged his head on the bus door, which served him right, I felt.

"Duggie! What's the idea creeping up on us, man?" he said, rubbing the back of his head.

"Hummph," I snorted. "You can hardly call it creeping with Rufie yapping on all cylinders."

Amanda smiled and cooed in Rufie's direction, and he promptly stopped barking and changed gears to vigorous tail wagging with a side of jumping.

"All right, all right," I said, trying to quiet him down. "The point is, what are you two doing here in the middle of the night? Haven't you got homes of your own?"

Amanda dropped her chin shyly and said, "We just wanted to get away from Jen, you know. She doesn't mind Eric, but, you know, she's all alone, and it just seems rude to be, like, a couple around her."

"Oh really? Well, if she's all alone it's certainly not my fault, is it? Come on out of there. Have you no respect for the concept of a covert operation? The whole point is you don't go out of your way to draw attention to it."

They stepped down and closed the bus door, which lowered the wattage in the immediate vicinity by about a thousand percent.

"That's a lot of pot you got there, Duggie. It seems like it's grown two feet since last week," said Eric.

"Shhh."

"What? There's nobody around for miles."

"You don't know that. There could be a hiker or a moonshiner."

"Do people still do that?"

"I don't know. They could, couldn't they?"

Eric shrugged. "I guess. If you're crazy enough to do this."

"This isn't crazy." I bristled. "The profit margin in this particular commodity has got moonshine beat by a mile."

"I'm gonna be rich," whispered Amanda.

"Yes, well. That's the plan," I said, leading them away from the bus. When we got back to my shack, I was afraid there might be an awkward moment if the lovebirds wanted to stick around and resume fondling. Fortunately they left without delay, and I was once again alone with my thoughts.

As thoughts go, they weren't altogether unpleasant. But lying in bed a short while later, I couldn't help thinking how much more pleasant it would have been to share them with Jenny before drifting off to dreamland. It was curious to hear Amanda describing Jenny alone. I never think of her alone. In my thoughts, she's always with me. If only she could see it that way.

CHAPTER 6

multo enim multoque quam hostem superare operosius
It is harder to conquer oneself than to conquer one's enemy.

There's a reason they don't hold parades in saunas. And it's not just the lack of leg room.

As I stood on the sidelines of Sycamore Street watching the high school marching band sweating all over their trombones, I felt a wave of pity mixed with pride. Even though they weren't wearing those big hats and heavy jackets that you see on the high-dollar parades on TV, they were clearly overdressed for the humid heat of a Rapidan July. The proper attire for our summers is the T-shirt and shorts, accompanied by flip flops or sneakers. No one under sixty wears anything else all summer long. So to see these kids straining under the weight of their tubas and bass drums, wearing uniforms of a hideous maroon and gold in the blazing sun while they clanged through a version of "Celebration," made me proud to be an American. And grateful that I had never taken up the clarinet.

I was waiting for the highlight of the parade, which, for me, would be the animal shelter's entry, in which I hoped to get a better glimpse of the mysterious Phoebe. Morris's assertion that this girl knew me had piqued my curiosity. Rapidan is not one of your densely populated centers of commerce where you can remain anonymous. Everyone knows everyone whether they like it or not. Therefore, if this girl said she knew me, I must, by the transitive property of something-or-other, know her. The question had been nagging at me, and I watched the passage of clowns and Cub Scouts with some impatience. Bring on the girls with cats was my feeling.

And lo, there she was. Blonde and perky as all get-out, and leading a large sullen black cat on a leash. Phoebe, if it was her, was wearing an ensemble more suited to the weather, and one that was designed to catch and hold the attention of the male spectators in the crowd. The shorts were tight, blue and shiny. The top was small, tasseled and full to capacity. A bright jewel sparkled in her navel, and her smile shone like an ad for tooth whitener. Cheers of appreciation rose from the men standing beside me, and I nearly joined them, but held back because, despite all the build-up, I looked at this girl and felt not an iota of recognition. I was baffled.

I stood for a while after the float passed, watching the tractors pulling haywagons loaded with sticky children, with my thoughts elsewhere. Normally, I would have shrugged off the incident. But, with the pot bus weighing on my mind, I was feeling more paranoid than usual. I wanted to know how this girl knew me, or why she said she did, if she didn't. I decided to look for her before I headed over to the field.

She was easy to find. Not easy to get to. Just easy to find. She was surrounded by a circle of wide-eyed boys and men while she passed out SPCA leaflets. As I edged nearer her eyes met mine, and I felt a bizarre spasm of vertigo. I clutched at the air and swayed for a second before regaining my composure. For, up close, it seemed to me there *was* something oddly familiar about this girl. I wondered if she was someone I had borrowed money from back in college. Before I had time to consult the records she was upon me. Literally.

"Duggie!" she cried, wrapping me in an embrace that left me breathless, in part due to the overpowering scent of watermelon and Juicy Fruit which hovered about her like some sort of pheromone signature. The ring of admirers regrouped around us, their envy almost palpable.

Not as palpable as Phoebe, of course, who was looking at me as if I were her long lost fiancé. I was, as before, baffled. I said, "Hello."

It wasn't the cleverest thing I could have said, I know, but she laughed as if I'd just told a really good one. She punched me playfully in the ribs, and said, "You don't remember me, do you?"

I considered lying. The truth seemed so tactless. But, I had a lot on my mind, and I couldn't be bothered. Lies take a lot more creativity and energy than the truth. "Honestly ... no. We met before?"

She grinned. "You wouldn't remember me. I was twelve. You were fourteen. I saw you at *certamen* in Charlottesville. You were awesome! You were like my hero for two years."

I couldn't say for certain, but at this point I may have blushed. Yet, it can't be denied. In my *certamen* years I was a god. A lesser god perhaps, in the pantheon of Latin geekdom, but, a god nonetheless.

"Oh. You saw me there."

"Yeah. I was on the team at my school. We were never very good. But we always cheered for you. Me and my girlfriends. You were so cute. And so smart!"

The past tense ... you noticed? I pretended I didn't. "Ah, well. That was a long time ago."

"Yeah. I guess you don't do that anymore."

"Nope."

She reached down and picked up the cat, which had been clawing at the leash this whole time as if hoping to somehow win through to freedom. "I'm not doing it either."

"Yes. Morris told me you're working at the shelter. That must be ... how is that?"

"It's great. I mean. It's not great, because it's sad sometimes, but I love animals, so it's good for me. And for my karma. I'm working on that a lot now. Trying to be a better person, you know? There's so much suffering in the world, and I just think if we all try to be more understanding and kind to one another it will make the world a better place. Don't you agree?"

I shrugged. "Of course. World peace. It's what we all want, isn't it? *beati pacifici* and all that."

Her eyes clouded uncertainly.

"Blessed are the peacemakers," I translated.

"Oh, right! Hah, hah, hah." Her laugh was exactly like sleigh bells. Uncanny. Made me feel like a god again. I shook myself, to realign the perception. Although, from a purely technical standpoint, this girl was undeniably adorable and apparently susceptible to my offbeat charm, my love for Jenny could brook no usurpers. There was room in my heart for one true love only—vis, Jennifer Leigh Carson. *Summa sedes non capit duos.* There wasn't room on the throne for another queen.

But, this girl was clearly smitten by the Moon charisma, and I felt the least I could do was let her down gently. To that end, I asked if she was planning on coming to watch the softball tournament. She said she was, in order to root for her good buddy

Amanda. I smiled and suggested that she might find her loyalties divided.

"Why is that?" she asked.

"Come to the game. You'll see," I said slyly. I could have told her that Amanda's team, even with Jenny on the roster, was going to have a tough time beating the Moonlighters as long as we had Eduardo. But, why spoil the moment? As I walked away I'm not ashamed to say that I felt that quiet glow of satisfaction that comes from hearing yourself praised. It matters not whether the praise is merited. It's always soothing to hear it.

The Ruritan field was swarming with players and spectators when I arrived twenty minutes later, having stopped off to devour the traditional pre-game hot dog on the way. The Moonlighters were slated to play the Swans in the second contest of the tournament's opening double header. The Firemen were due to face the Sandblasters in the first game.

I looked for a spot on the grassy bank that serves as a sort of *au natural* bleacher fixture. The upper regions of this bank enjoy the added blessing of dappled shade from a hefty white oak, and those of us who have weathered a few of these steamy all day events understand the market value of shade. I spied an unoccupied stretch next to Witty, who was, I noticed with concern, sitting close to Rosalie. I hurried up to put a damper on this.

"Hey. How do they look?"

Witty turned from Rosalie reluctantly and said, "Who?"

"The Sandblasters, who else?"

He frowned slightly and said, "I don't know. I haven't really been watching them."

I sat down and addressed my remarks to Rosalie, giving her a meaningful glance as I did so, in the hope that she would be more reasonable than Witt. She smiled at me in the usual manner, as if I were a presumptuous child begging for candy.

"That pitcher looks like he's got some heat," I observed, trying to get the ball rolling. Witt said nothing but kept staring at Rosalie with an intensity that bordered on the indecent.

"That's a good arm on that center fielder," I said. Even as I said this, trying to draw a response from Witt, I couldn't help noticing that the Sandblasters did, in fact, have a kind of snap and precision in their warm-up that set them apart from the local boys. On the sidelines, where a dugout would have been if this were a real ball field, the Firemen, led by Roy Spooner and Curtis Branch, were tossing a ball back and forth in a desultory way, making an unconvincing show of not checking out their opponents. There was an eerie quiet on the field. None of the banter and loose chatter that usually precedes the first game of the tournament.

When the courthouse bell chimed once across town, Art Claypool, a welder by trader and the umpire by virtue of his imposing form and implacable nature, stepped onto the field and blew his aoogah horn to signal the official start. The marching band rustled into formation behind the backstop and began a lusty, quick time version of "The Star Spangled Banner," which is the only way to go with that sorry tune if you ask me. Play it fast and put us out of our misery. Too many times these celebrity performers stretch and strain the melody as if trying to prove that they can make it sound like music, but they never do. It's a terrible song. Everyone knows "God Bless America" should be the national anthem. Even the atheists. But I digress.

Once the last cymbal crashed, the umpire cried "Play ball!" And DK and his team trotted on the field like storm troopers in baseball hats. Roy Spooner stepped up to bat, with a last pointless tug on his pants as if to coax them up above the beer belly. He tapped his bat on the plate once, and the next second something whizzed across it and went "smock!" in the catcher's glove.

"Steerike one," said Art.

Roy stepped back and frowned at him. Then he bent his knees a bit and faced the pitcher, a tall corn-fed-looking lad whose arms moved like pistons. Another blistering pitch streaked by Roy. "Steerike two," said Art.

Roy glared at him, and Art shrugged. "Don't look at me," he muttered.

Roy set his jaw and squinted out at the pitcher. He raised the bat above his shoulders. There was a moment of dead silence and then, "smock!" The ball was in the catcher's mitt again, and, I swear, I never even saw it. There's no way Roy could have hit it. He stood there for a few seconds before turning and walking back to the bench.

The crowd shifted uneasily. Everyone likes Roy. It didn't seem right that he didn't even get to swing at a ball in his first at bat of the season. I glanced over at Witt and was relieved to see that he had finally started paying attention. "Whoah," he whispered. "Where'd that guy come from?"

"Maybe he's one of the Cannon rejects," I said.

"Man." Witt shook his head. "That's not right."

In less than two minutes, the next two batters struck out. Only one of them even managed to swing at a ball. No one clapped when the Sandblasters came in for their at bat. The writing was already on the wall, and the Firemen knew what it said, even without their reading glasses.

The first Sandblaster to take the plate looked like the Hulk's younger brother. He smacked a home run on the first pitch and jogged around the bases without even a grin. The crowd was beginning to mutter.

The second hitter hit a line drive that tore between first and second base and had the Firemen scurrying after the ball like slapstick clowns. By the time they managed to retrieve it and get it to the plate, the runner had loped in for run number two.

The next up at bat was DK himself. The Dark Lord. Someone we knew. A few boos erupted from the crowd. I peered past Rosalie to see where they were coming from. They had a distinctly feminine quality, and I thought I saw Phoebe down in front with her hands cupped by her mouth. I was pleased to think she understood the core values of the game.

Whether or not the boos affected DK, he missed the first pitch, and a chorus of cheers greeted his whiff. He stepped back from the plate, adjusted his hat, wiggled his shoulders and stepped up again. The second pitch he struck foul. The ball sailed up behind us, going out of sight in the oak tree. A couple of kids scampered off to retrieve it, but, because this was the big time tournament of the year, Art had a spare ball in his pocket. He carried this out to Wendell Frink, the Firemen's pitcher, and it looked like he may have uttered a word or two. I'd like to think he was giving advice, even though, from a purely legal standpoint, that might not be how it's done in the big leagues. But this is Rapidan. We don't care so much about playing by the rules as making sure the game is fair and fun. Rules are made to be interpreted.

Art returned to his post, and Wendell took a deep breath. Then he threw a pitch which we don't see often around these parts. Most of the pitching in the dirtball softball league comes in two flavors. You have your chocolate—as fast as you can throw it as close to over the plate as you can manage—and your vanilla, a kind of loopy version of the above. Sliders, curve balls, sinkers, these are pitches we hear about in the sports news, but we rarely encounter them. But Wendell, who had played ball at Rapidan High and acquitted himself honorably, must have retained a few brain cells from those years, because the next selection he offered to Doyle Krump's bat was a sinking slider that wound its way to the plate like a snake with a fresh rat stuck in its throat.

DK had to adjust his swing in midrotation and managed to just nick the ball so that it trickled toward Wendell. DK started pelting toward first base but the catcher, Mickey Brewster, as nimble as he is pugnacious, scuttled out, grabbed the ball and managed to pick off Krump. Full-throated cheers rewarded this play, and for about thirty seconds we felt refreshed by the nectar of hope. Then the next Sandblaster came up to bat and promptly hit another home run. We settled back on the grass and tried to act like we didn't care.

At the end of the first inning the Sandblasters were ahead 5-0. The remainder of the game followed the pattern. Three up, three down for the Firemen. Hits flying out of the park for the Sandblasters. By the end of the sixth inning it was 14-0, and there was talk of invoking the slaughter rule. But Roy and Curtis refused. Their stubbornness was rewarded with one shining moment in the bottom of the eighth, when a casual catch by one of the Sandblasters resulted in an error which allowed a runner to get on base. Then a courageous stolen base, a daring bunt, and a fluke single to right field allowed the Firemen the dignity of scoring one run. There was cheering, but it was grim even so.

By the end the Sandblasters had buried the Firemen, 26 to 1. And to make it worse, they left the field without shaking hands.

We tried to focus on the game ahead, us against the Swans. As we walked down to the field Witt said, "You know, I never thought I'd say this, but, compared to Krump's gang? Shitley doesn't seem that evil anymore."

I nodded, looking around. Krump's henchmen had already disappeared. No sticking around to watch the other teams for them, I guess. No doubt they had other parades to rain upon.

I saw Glory's head bobbing through the crowd, and a moment later she came up to us, her face aglow with righteous wrath.

"Who let those guys in the tournament? Who's responsible for this? I was just talking to Martin Fisher, and he looked like he was going to cry. That's just wrong!"

I patted her on the shoulder. "Don't worry. We'll find a way to fix them."

"Phah! You couldn't fix scrambled eggs!"

I didn't see the connection between my cooking skills and the game of softball, but I could see that Glory was worked up, and I let it go. When her passions are aroused, she often resorts to culinary slurs.

"Trust me. I have a plan." I assured her with another pat. She swatted my hand away.

"You and your plans. As if I didn't have enough to worry about."

I might have gone into this further, but I had a game to play and no time to counsel. Plus, Jenny was on the mound. God, presumably was in his heaven, and, for a few pleasant hours, all was right with the world.

I was almost sorry we had to beat them. And, not to ruin the suspense, but, in the interest of moving right along, I must report that the Moonlighters did, in the end, prevail over the Swans. But, it was close, 6-3. And, more importantly, the game was played in the spirit for which the tournament is justly famed. Merriment and hi-jinks. Good sportsmanship and fair play. Patience when the second ball disappeared in the blackberry thicket at the far edge of left field, Since we had already lost the other ball to an over-eager Labrador who ran off with it, play more or less came to a standstill for fifteen minutes while the intrepid ball boys scratched their way into the thorny tangle to retrieve it.

It was a long, lazy game, in other words. Full of good-natured insults and back and forth chatter. I saw Jenny roll her eyes in disbelief when Kevin skulked into the outfield. "I didn't know weasels could catch," she said. Her surprise at seeing Kevin was nothing compared to the shock value of Darren's pitching. Only a few people outside our team had ever seen the kid hurl, and I could tell by the way Jenny stared after the first ball smoked across the plate that she was rattled. Luckily, Darren somehow managed to avoid hitting all but one batter, and fortunately it was Lydell Williams, who has a kind of natural beer belly buffer that prevented serious injury.

Word had gotten out about Eduardo's batting before the game, of course, so no one was surprised when he hit a triple off one of Jenny's best pitches. But you could tell she wasn't really upset about it. If you love the game, you can't help admiring someone like Eduardo, even when he's playing against you.

No one said anything about the clinical display that had preceded our game. It was as if all of us had witnessed a killing, and we didn't want the mob to come after us. But, when I shook hands with Jenny at the end, I could see it in her eyes—a kind of bruised look. She gripped my hand a little longer than usual and leaned her luscious lips in close to my face, and for a moment I couldn't breath, but then she whispered, "You be careful tomorrow."

Well, I hadn't really expected a kiss, of course. Because Jenny and I, you know. That's not how it is, much as I dream about it. But, I realized with a rush of warmth, that she was worried about me, and if that was true, then maybe she was no longer pissed off about me hiring Amanda for the bus. So, something good had some out of the Firemen's' massacre. It just goes to show: *post nubila Phoebus*—every cloud has a silver lining.

Jenny was walking off the field and I was standing there, basking in the afterglow of her face so close to mine, when suddenly there was a blonde blur in my peripheral vision and something hit my chest.

"Woof!" I gasped as the air went out of me.

"Oh, Duggie! You were great! I never knew you were such an athlete! When you caught that ball and threw it to get that guy out? That was amazing!"

When she stopped to breathe, Phoebe smiled up at me with such candid affection that it would have taken a soul more churlish than mine to crush her innocent enthusiasm. So I smiled back and murmured something about "it takes a team" et cetera, but I can't deny, the flood of praise from girlish lips is something new to me. Usually, when girls talk to me, the tone of voice tends toward the sarcastic and impatient. I'm used to it. I didn't quite know how to react to this fulsome warmth. I glanced over her head a bit nervously and nearly bit my tongue when my eyes met Jenny's. She was staring at me, or rather, at Phoebe and me, and the look on her face was one I'd never seen there before. I pulled myself loose from Phoebe's arms and tried to shrug my shoulders at Jenny, thus conveying a "girls-will-be-girls" sentiment which I expected would bring a smile to her face. But, strangely, it didn't. She looked at me for another second or two, then turned and walked away. I would have spent some time analyzing this, but Phoebe had other plans.

"Come on. I want to buy you a beer," she said, grabbing my hand and leading me away. I tried to see where Jenny had gone, but there were too many people milling around. So in the end I decided to be civil. Phoebe might be an airhead, but that was no reason to be rude. I followed her to the tavern.

The Tin Toad makes up in attitude what it lacks in style. There are those who won't patronize the place, claiming that the dim light hides an entire ecosphere of bacteria and villainy. But I say, who wants to see those things? And besides, no one goes there for the decor. It's all about the jukebox, which has selections ranging from early Hank Williams and Benny Goodman to latter day Bob

Dylan and Death Cab for Cutie, with a substantial helping of world music and Motown B-sides. Something for everyone.

Well, almost everyone. Phoebe flipped rapidly through the playlist and poonched her lower lip out in disappointment because there was nothing from Madonna.

"I know what you're thinking. She's passé and shallow, like me." Phoebe said this with a pixie grin that made it difficult to know whether or not she was kidding or fishing for a compliment. I complied with the latter since it seemed the right thing to do.

"What do you mean, shallow? No one who has ever loved Latin could be called shallow."

She batted her eyes, a thing I didn't think women did in real life. "Oh, that's sweet, Duggie. But, you know, I never really was very good at Latin."

"I'm sure that's not true. Besides, the important thing is not whether you were any good at it, but that you appreciated it at all. Not everyone does."

Her eyes shone at me, speaking volumes, I imagine, though it was kind of hard to read in the dim light. It was also hard to talk, since, what with the jukebox playing and the clientele attempting to converse above it, the din was substantial. I glanced around and noticed that a fair number of the Firemen seemed to be drowning their sorrows successfully. As a team captain, I couldn't help but shake my head for them. Wiser heads would have counseled going easy on the intoxicants on the eve of another game, but, of course, the next day they would only be playing the Swans. Perhaps the Firemen felt they could afford to unwind.

I felt no such liberty to indulge in the traditional lubricants, knowing that the next day the Moonlighters would face DK's gang of thugs on the field of battle. I frowned as I contemplated the coming contest. I'm an easy going sort of guy. Ask anyone. But I couldn't help feeling a tad aggrieved that our normally lighthearted event was being blighted by this Krump. Something should be done. I just couldn't think what, off the top of my head.

"Duggie? Are you okay?"

I glanced down into Phoebe's anxious face. I shook my head. "I'm fine. Or that is, I will be. But I think I'd better call it a night."

The sparkle in Phoebe's eyes fizzled. She nodded sadly and fell upon me, wrapping her arms around me in a hug that very nearly revived me. But, I told myself, this was not the time, the place, nor, in spite of her obvious charms, the girl, for me, so I said good night and left.

It had been an unsettling day, and I wasted no time in lighting up a healing joint the moment I got onto the mountain road. Despite the brave face I had put on for the crowd at the Toad, in my heart I was, frankly, quaking at the prospect of tomorrow's game. However, such is the power of the fragrant herb, that by the time I pulled into the gravel drive I was feeling, if not utterly carefree, a pleasant detachment, more in tune with my inner Buddha as you might say. When I turned off the engine, I sat in the truck, listening to the cicadas and the birds doing whatever it is they do in the dark, and I suppose I was lost in thought, because I didn't notice the crunching footsteps on the gravel until they were almost upon me. I jerked my head toward the window, prepared to deal with this intruder in no uncertain terms. I was getting fed up with the infestation of uninvited late night guests, who seemed to feel that the welcome mat was always out at the House of Duggie.

"Do you mind?" I began, then stopped as the scent of her skin hit me. It's like ripe melons, or peaches. Normally, the visual input kind of overrides the impact, but here in the dark, the smell of Jenny's body so close to mine made my brain melt. "Jenny?"

"Where have you been? I've been waiting here over an hour."

I was shocked. First by her tone, which suggested a degree of proprietary attitude that took me by surprise; and second, that she had waited, more than an hour, for me! I started to explain about having stopped at the Toad, and she interrupted my babbling to ask, "Were you alone?"

I tried to gauge her expression. The tone of her voice held a *soupçon* of hostility, but I put that down to her previous snit over my luring her sister into a life of crime, as she thought.

"One is never alone at the Toad," I began, striking the light note, as is my way.

"Don't give me that. Who were you with?"

I bit my tongue to stifle the impulse to correct her grammar, knowing how she hates that in the best of times, and this wasn't one of them. "Um, let me see," I said. "Randall was there, and Art. A bunch of the Firemen were drowning their collective sorrows. Oh, and Phoebe."

A fraught silence followed. I may have been imagining it, but I thought I could hear her nostrils flaring. Maybe it was the pot.

"Phoebe's the blonde?"

"Um. Yes. I believe her hair is blonde. Though I couldn't tell you whether it's natural or not—"

"Duggie! You're rambling. You're such a bad liar. I don't know why you even bother to try with me. I'm on your side, remember?"

I beamed. I wasn't really paying attention to her words per se. I just couldn't help feeling happy that she was there, in the dark, sharing her thoughts with me. We belonged together. It was so obvious.

"I'm just worried about you."

"Really?" I was touched. Here I had thought she had come to continue bawling me out over her sister, and instead, she had come out of affection. I wondered if I could get away with a hug.

"Of course, you moron. Did you see those guys today? They're like the Borg. Cold, merciless machines. They're not just going to kick your ass. They're out for blood."

I stopped smiling. Clearly, she wasn't in the mood. "I know, I know. I don't know whose idea it was to let them in the tournament."

"It doesn't matter now. What matters is, you have to be on your guard tomorrow."

I shrugged. I mean, I wasn't planning to get stoned before the game. What more did she want?

"I'm serious Duggie! You can't just smoke a reefer in the outfield and hope they won't run over you with their cleats."

"Were they wearing cleats?" In Rapidan an occasional barefoot has been seen on the field, but never anything approaching technical gear.

Jenny threw her hands up in the air. "I don't know! That's not the point. The point is, you have to promise me that you're not going to do anything stupid tomorrow. I don't want you to get hurt."

My beam returned.

"For better or for worse, my baby sister is counting on you to pull off this insane pot scheme, and if you wind up in the hospital she's going to be left holding the bag. So help me, Duggie, if you make this any worse I'll kill you myself."

I rolled the window up, just to put myself out of reach while I collected my thoughts, which, it must be said, were not as light as they had been moments before. So. It wasn't concern for me that had motivated her after-hours visit. This shouldn't surprise me. But, as so often happens when I'm a bit stoned, I had allowed my sunny optimism to override my stoic nature. Jenny did not, and never had, loved me. She cared about Amanda. This was only natural. And commendable. I sighed. Back to business. I rolled down the window. Jenny was standing there with her arms folded and her lips set in a tense line.

"It's okay," I began.

"You idiot! It's not okay. It's not even close to okay! But I'm just warning you, if you let yourself get maimed tomorrow, I will never forgive you."

With that, she stormed off into the night and I was alone with my thoughts again.

CHAPTER 7

Ignis aurum probat, miseria fortes viros.
Fire tests gold; adversity strong men.

Well, if you were worried that, after a day full to the brim with disturbing developments, I would be unable to get the kind of restful sleep that makes such a difference in the quality of one's life, you can rest easy. I certainly did. And woke to the second day of the tournament positively glowing. For, you see, despite Jenny's gloomy outlook and the admittedly sobering spectacle of DK's henchmen demolishing the Firemen, I felt reasonably confident that the Moonlighters would fare better against the goons.

Not because I have unrealistic expectations of our team's talents, but because I know DK, and if there's one thing that goeth before the fall, he's got it in spades. Especially after serving the Firemen a super-sized order of humiliation in yesterday's game, DK would be expecting to crush the life out of the Moonlighters. But since the Sandblasters didn't stick around to see game number two of the tournament, they missed out on seeing Eduardo at bat or, more importantly, the chance to scout Darren's pitching.

Of course, the beauty of Darren's pitching is that scouting is ineffective anyway. It's not as if you can look at his windup and know what kind of pitch is coming. I don't think Darren knows.

So, considering this, I felt fairly confident. In all likelihood, the bad guys might win anyway. But possibly not without a few bruises and contusions.

I breakfasted lightly on a few slices of peanut butter toast and drove to the field, arriving just in time to see Jenny throw the first pitch against the Firemen. It was a thing of beauty. Not unlike herself. And though Roy Spooner swung with gusto, it didn't get him anywhere, inasmuch as the bat rose up while the ball sank under it. You could see Roy wasn't happy about it, but he tapped the bat on the plate and stepped up for pitch number two with something like a determined grin on his face. When he managed to tip the ball on the next pitch he scurried to first base just ahead of the ball. A cheer went up from the Firemen supporters, and the mood on the field assumed the familiar aspect of a regular potluck supper, where everyone brings something and it's all good and nobody talks about diets.

It was clear halfway through the first inning that the Swans had the edge on the Firemen. Whether it was because of Jenny's superior pitching, or the fact that some of the Firemen had a hard time keeping their eyes on the ball what with all the women on the Swan roster, I couldn't say. But I'll say this for Shitley, he may be tightwad when it comes to employee benefits, but there was no denying that the Swans' T-shirts and hats lent a tone to the proceedings that you don't often see in Rapidan. The hats were dark purple with *Swans* in white script. The shirts were white with a dark purple swan logo on the front, and the way those shirts fit some of the girls was enough to drive a man to poetry.

Still, the play was competitive, and the score was tied 2-2 at the seventh inning stretch. But then, in the bottom of the eighth Babe hit a line drive into center field that drove home Mindy, who broke off flirting with Curtis Fletcher, the Firemen's second baseman, to score. Then, with Babe on first, Jenny came up to bat and bunted, which allowed Babe to hustle to second. Eric was up next and struck out. The blush of embarrassment on his cheeks went from pink to pinker when Amanda said something to him as he slunk back to the bench. I felt for him. I guessed she had whispered some words of encouragement in his ear, but the time for tenderness isn't on the ballfield, and I suspect even Eric knows this.

However, the spike in Eric's humiliation came moments later when Amanda socked a home run high and deep into left field. The Swans leapt to their feet and there was much tooting of horns and flapping of arms, as if the entire team were preparing for liftoff.

From that point it was pretty much all over for the Firemen. They played out the last inning, but you could see their hearts weren't in it. The Swans were gracious in victory, and a number of the Firemen seemed to find comfort in the hugs freely given by the Swans' female members. Eric remained aloof from the proceedings. Ordinarily I would have taken him aside and offered some sound words of advice to prevent him from making a bigger ass of himself. But I had more pressing concerns.

While the Swans' celebration moved off the field, I looked around to gather the Moonlighters together for a little warm-up. But, I have to admit, when I caught sight of DK flexing his biceps in the parking lot, it sent a chill right through me. He looked like one of your large, economy-size Vikings just out for a spot of pillaging. I turned away and the first person I saw, I kid you not, was Kevin. A weasel in human form. And I felt it keenly that here, in stark metaphorical style, was the haiku, if you will, of the upcoming athletic contest:

Furry mammals creep.
Water buffaloes tap dance.

There is no encore.

I sighed, a bit peevishly. It was bad enough having Shitley trying to ruin the tournament with his fancy shirts and press coverage. Add DK and his storm troopers to the mix, and it almost didn't seem worth the effort.

"Hey, you okay? You look like you're worried about something."

I shook myself. Phoebe's lustrous blue eyes were shining on me with an intensity that made me wish I'd brought sunglasses.

"Oh, no. I'm fine. Just ... donning the mental armor, so to speak."

Her forehead puckered. "Huh?"

"Getting ready for the game," I added.

"Oh right. Of course. Those guys look really mean." She frowned over at the Sandblasters, who were doing some brisk calisthenics, barking out numbers as they performed them. Oh, for a pellet gun, I mused.

I adopted a winning smile and assured Phoebe that the Moonlighters would not be eclipsed by any team, no matter how mean, and she seemed cheered by my words. I kept the smile pasted on my face until she had finished giving me a good luck hug and walked away. Only then did the inner terror reassert itself. I glanced back at DK's gang. The azure sky yielded no hint of a rain cloud. Nature never steps up when it counts.

I gathered the team together, and in a few terse words told them that I didn't expect anyone to risk injury to win the game. "I hate to say this," I said, "but I don't know if we have much of a chance against these guys."

"Well hell, whyn't we forfeit?"

I looked around to see who had said this, but I knew, before I caught a glimpse of his matted dreadlocks, who had spoken. The other players retreated like pleasure crafts yielding to a barge, and

Phillip Wray pushed through. Photon, as he is more commonly known, is the 21st century equivalent of a loose cannon. Not a precision instrument, but useful in the right circumstances. He trained his glassy eyes on me, and I took a deep breath before I replied. One wants to be measured in responding to Photon. He's not tall, but he makes up in breadth for what he lacks in height, and he's like one of those big dogs that don't know their own strength—as liable to injure you with affection as with animosity. So, I smiled thinly and said, "We can't forfeit. Glory's counting on us."

"That's her problem. If she cares so much, why ain't she out here?"

"She's here. She's in the stands, ready to cheer us on."

"Well that don't buy me beer. Who gives a crap about cheering?"

At this range I could tell that Photon had already been fueling his inner torpedo on the aforementioned beverage. There was a light in his eyes that reminded me of the line by Horace, *aut insanit homo aut versus facit* — the man is either mad or he is composing verses. Photon at times has waxed poetic, but I didn't think this was going to be one of those times.

"Listen, I know this looks bad. And those guys look tough. But if we go out there and give it our best, we'll have nothing to be ashamed of."

"That's crap Duggie, and you know it." Photon fixed me with his steely stare. Admittedly, the steel seemed to be slowly revolving, but it was definitely metallic. Or perhaps Metallica. Once a head banger always a head banger.

I shrugged my shoulders and said, "Listen, men—"

"*Excusez moi!*" Rosalie interrupted.

"Sorry. Listen, team. I won't lie. This is going to be a rough game. But remember, *audentes fortuna iuvat.*"

"What?" Photon grunted.

"Fortune favors the brave. Virgil said that, and he was no fool. I'm not asking you to work a miracle. Just do your best and I'll be proud of you."

The expressions on their faces weren't exactly as inspired as I might have hoped, but at least they didn't walk off the field. And Rosalie was smiling. I focused on that as we went in for the coin toss.

The game that followed ... how shall I put it? Let's just say that if you've ever wondered what it would be like to experience artillery practice from the point of view of the target, you could have written the paper without purchasing the Cliff notes by the end of the third inning. The Sandblasters were up by about ten runs at that point, if memory serves. I can't be sure. The ego has its own cloaking device. I do remember the one bright moment in the entire fiasco, which occurred sometime after a hailstorm of fly balls had been falling on center field like a malevolent meteor shower. Something caused Photon to snap. It may have been the sight of Rosalie's tear-stained face after she had been knocked off her feet by one of DK's thugs on his way around the bases. I don't know what actually yanked Photon's chain from the wall, but I do know this, when DK was standing on second base, complacently awaiting the hit that would send him in to score, Photon threw something, a rock perhaps, or maybe it was just a hard clod of dirt. Whatever it was, it struck DK below the belt with a force that dropped him to the ground where he proceeded to writhe and groan for several moments during which the rest of us basked in his suffering. I'm not saying it was our finest moment. But, there are times when only the enemy's pain can soothe our own. This was one of those times.

When the debacle concluded the Sandblasters disappeared without a victory cheer, and the rest of us limped to the side of the field and contemplated the dirt in silence. I can't deny, I had never felt so whipped. We didn't get a single run. We only managed to get two men on base in the entire game. And in the eerie silence of the aftermath the mood was so dark that the only light was that which seemed to be coming off Photon. He had the look of a nuclear device that hadn't been taking its medication.

Suddenly, something warm and wonderful wrapped around my shoulders. I looked up and, I'm not ashamed to say, I nearly wept with gratitude as Jenny kissed me gently on the cheek. "Tough luck slugger," she whispered. "Don't let it get to you."

Such is the power of love that at that instant I would cheerfully have challenged a squadron of DKs to a rematch. Thankfully, the moment passed. Jenny removed her arm and turned to the rest of the team. "Hey you guys," she said. "Don't worry about today. Those bums think they own us now. But they don't know it all. We can still take them down."

"Only if we can use a machine gun," Witty growled.

A half-hearted ripple of laughter met this remark, like signs of life in a cadaver.

"No, seriously," said Jenny. "These guys have skills, and they're strong. But we're smart, and we've got skills too. We just need to find a way to put them off their game. We've got to get into their heads."

"How are we supposed to do that?" Randall said. "Get 'em stoned?"

Several people looked at me. I ignored them, but I couldn't help noticing that Kevin brightened up at this suggestion. His upper lip twitched in a way that enhanced his uncanny resemblance to a rodent who sniffs hidden cheese.

"That's a good idea," he said.

I frowned. "No. No, it's not, for more reasons than I care to go into. But Jenny's right. We need to think outside the box to beat these guys."

"Pheh. I'm getting a drink. If you guys want to talk strategy, I'll be at The Toad." Photon lumbered off the field, and it seemed as good an idea as any, so we all followed him.

Jenny lingered behind and walked beside me. After the beating we'd taken, I appreciated her loyalty more than ever. Here she was, on the eve of facing those same goons on the field of battle, and she was with me—we were allies fighting the same evil horde, tag-team fashion. My bruises ached less just being close to her.

"You did okay today, Duggie."

"You think?"

"You didn't get hit by the ball. You didn't break any limbs."

"Huh. I guess it could have been worse."

Jenny pursed her lips. "There's gotta be a way."

"A way to beat them?"

"Yeah."

I sighed. "I don't know, Jen. I didn't see any signs of weakness. They're like Cylons."

We were almost at the Toad by now. Jenny reached for my hand. My throat got tight, and I forgot what we were talking about. She leaned closer and said, "Listen, Duggie. Just remember. This is Rapidan County. That means there's only one rule, right?"

I stared at her perfect mouth, imagining my lips touching it.

"Duggie? Are you listening to me? What's the only rule?"

I shook myself. The only rule? Right. I know this one. "There are no rules."

"That's right. Don't you forget it. You'll think of something."

I nodded. But then she hugged me, and my brain kind of melted, and I couldn't tell you what happened right after that because it took me a while to return to earth. But ah. It was worth it.

By the time I came down, the proceedings inside the Toad were well underway. I couldn't say that I heard any brilliant ideas being bandied about, but it was clear from the volume of the discussion that there was no shortage of opinion. I looked around the room, trying to decide which conversation to join. Among the options were a group gathered around Photon, who appeared to be urging them to unbridled mayhem, clanging his beer can on the table and chanting something that sounded like "blast the bastards." I ruled this group out quickly and turned to option B, a cluster of mostly Swan players who appeared to be in high spirits, with Jenny at their center. I began to move toward them without thinking until my legs grew numb at the sight of an insidiously handsome stranger seated next to Jenny. The guy had that kind of lean, chiseled look that girls go for, and his eyes, the dark smoldering kind, were glued on Jenny. I felt a spasm of nausea.

As the room reeled about me I turned and saw a dark corner made even darker by the expression on Eduardo's face. He was sitting alone at a table for two, glaring at his beer as if it had insulted his mustache. The sight chilled me, and made me realize I couldn't allow my feelings for Jenny to obscure the mission, which was to find a way to hobble the Sandblasters. Any plan I could hope to hatch would need Eduardo's cooperation. He was the only one on our team who got a hit every time he came to bat. It wasn't his fault that the Sandblasters had outstanding fielders. I pushed my way through the crowd and sunk onto the seat across from him.

"Hey Eduardo. Tough game today," I began.

He raised his eyes to mine, and I was unnerved by the level of distrust I saw in them.

"Don't worry. We'll find a way to beat them in the final," I said, with more conviction than I felt.

He shrugged and looked across the room. I followed his gaze and saw Rosalie laughing at a table with Eric, Amanda and Witty. I looked back at Eduardo. It didn't take a genius to follow his train of thought. I frowned across the room at Witty, trying to catch his eye, but he was staring at Rosalie with such undisguised lust, it was no wonder the Cuban chef was stewing.

I decided to go break things up and remind Witty of the mission. "Excuse me. I'll be right back," I said to Eduardo. I worked my way across the room to the lovebirds' table and sat next to Witty.

"Hey! What's the idea?" I whispered in his ear. It wasn't a real whisper, of course. More one of those shouting whispers on account of the din.

He turned his head slightly in my direction and said, "What are you doing here?"

"That's what I'm asking you," I responded.

"It's none of your business what I'm doing," he replied.

I scowled at him, not that he noticed. His eyes were glued on Rosalie, who was looking radiant as all get-out. "Listen, Witt. Eduardo's over there, and he's getting upset seeing you here with, you know . . ."

"So what? We're going to lose anyway. Let him quit. Why should I care?"

"I thought you were my friend."

"Duggie, this isn't about you." Witty turned on me with an exasperated expression. "Can't you get it in your head? I've found the woman of my dreams. I'm not going to back off just because some neurotic chef has delusions of romance. She likes me! I've got a shot. I'm not backing off. That's final Duggie. Now beat it." He turned his back on me, and I sat there with my mouth open and my mind dazed for about a minute. Then I got up and went back to Eduardo.

I decided to venture a slight deception. "Those guys are a riot," I began, smiling ingratiatingly.

"What is a riot?" Eduardo's voice rumbled like a dump truck.

"Oh, you know. A barrel of laughs, a hoot, a ..." I clammed up, silenced by the glint in Eduardo's eyes. He didn't look amused.

"I think maybe I quit this team."

"No! No. You don't want to do that." I tried to remain calm. Talk him off the ledge. "Listen, is it because of Rosalie? Because, I know she likes you. She told me so. She's just shy. And friendly. Friendly and shy. A little of each, like half and half, you know?" I was babbling. But the important thing in these crisis situations is to keep up the flow, the lifeline of jabber. "And that guy Witty? Don't pay any attention to him. You have to understand, he flirts with every woman he meets. It's like breathing for him. Doesn't mean anything. He's a confirmed bachelor, like me."

Eduardo shifted his eyes to meet mine, and a quiver of uneasiness went through me. He turned back to look at the table where Rosalie and Witt were laughing, and his face went blank. I followed his gaze. Amanda and Eric were still cooing into each other's ears at the table, but Rosalie and Witt had disappeared. I tried to no avail to catch Eduardo's sleeve as he went charging toward the door. I scuttled after him. Out in the parking lot the night was dark, but the Toad's neon sign lit up the shadows well enough that there was no mistaking the sight of Witty and Rosalie locked in one of those Hollywood-style smooches. Eduardo braked so suddenly I ran into him. I would have apologized, but, somehow, I knew he hadn't even noticed my impact. He stood glaring at the happy couple for about half a minute, then he turned on his heel and stormed off into the night.

I should have run after him, I suppose. But really. Would you? There was no positive spin I could put on that revolting display of animal lust. Honestly. As if the shellacking we had just take from

DK's team wasn't enough. Now I had to find a way to keep from losing our star batter. We might be able to beat the Firemen without him. But I doubted it.

I trudged back into the Toad and sat down at the bar.

"Hey sailor, you come here often?"

My heart jumped off the floor and began to rumba. Jenny was still wearing her Swan team shirt. I don't know why women waste thousands on high fashion. "Hi. I thought you'd be home in bed by now, resting up for the big game." I said.

Jenny shrugged. I got goosebumps. Every little thing she does, you know? "Ah, Duggie. I figure there's no point in getting worked up about it. After watching those guys steamroll over the Moonlighters, even though you have Eduardo and wild man Darren, I realized there's no way the Swans can win. Almost half our team is women. And they're good ball players. But," she shook her head. "I'm not like you, Duggie. I'm a realist. We're going to lose. So I might as well have a couple of beers."

I nodded. I could see her point. But, the mention of green-eyed Eduardo reminded me of the sight of Jenny chatting with the hunk of unknown origin and I couldn't stop myself from asking, "Say, who was that guy I saw you with?"

She looked puzzled for an instant. "Oh, you mean that guy at the bar? I don't know. Just another sleazeball looking for someone to squeeze."

"So you ...?"

She laughed. "I told him he'd have to wait till after the tournament. I need to stay focused." She watched my face for a few seconds before she grabbed my knee and said, "I'm kidding! Come on, Duggie. You know me better than that."

The touch of her hand on my knee made it hard for me to speak for a moment, but when I regained control of my vocal chords I returned to the topic at hand, vis. our hot-tempered star slugger.

"Say, Jenny, about Eduardo?"

"Yeah?"

In a few terse words I told her about the recent unfortunate scene, and she immediately grasped the seriousness of the situation. She mused for about half a second, and then one of those amazing smiles flashed across her face, and when I recovered from it I had to ask her to repeat what she'd said.

"I said, I know what you need. What Eduardo needs. It's obvious."

"It is?"

"Of course. When a guy gets his heart smashed, the best way to make him forget is another girl."

"Well, sure. But ... do you have someone in mind? I mean, we kind of need one overnight."

"I know just the girl."

"Who?"

"You'll see."

"Jenny, I'm afraid Eduardo isn't even going to show up for the game tomorrow."

"You tell him there's a secret reason he has to play tomorrow."

"Why would he buy that?"

"Because he's got that Latin-American romance gene. He's human. He'll be curious. And besides, what else has he got to do?"

"I hope you're right." I studied her face. Her eyes were twinkling as if she were some Japanese anime character. "You won't give me a hint?"

"No, it's more fun this way. Trust me. I know someone who's been dying to get to know Eduardo, and he's going to be pleased to meet her."

I shrugged. "Okay. And this mystery woman will be at the game tomorrow?"

"She'll be there before the game. To meet him. Tell him that."

I was feeling mildly hopeful following this talk as I stepped out into the muggy night. The stars were twinkling above in the velvet firmament, as the fellow said. The night air held a rich mixture of honeysuckle and wild roses. If only I'd had the right girl to share it with, I could have been more than a little content at that moment. But then someone broke the mood, as they so often do. In this case it was Amanda, bubbling up beside me like some blonde geyser.

"Oh, Duggie. Isn't it a beautiful night! Eric had to leave, but I stayed because Jenny is giving me a ride, and I wanted to talk to you."

"Oh?" I wasn't feeling particularly chatty with this carefree Carson sibling. It might be unreasonable, but I held her partly responsible for the whole Witty-slash-Rosalie thing this evening. She should have prevented them from sneaking outside. But I remained civil.

"Yeah. I was talking with Mindy? You know? The pet-sitter? She's on our team?"

I nodded, thus answering all these non-binding questions with one economical motion. Perhaps she had a point that would be revealed eventually.

"Well, tonight? That guy Kevin? The ratty one? He was hitting on Mindy in the bar—"

"Kevin was hitting on Mindy?" I hated to adopt her conversational style, but truly I was taken aback to think that someone as repellant as Kevin would have the nerve to foist his attentions on a girl like Mindy.

"Yeah. And she was being nice? Because she is? And they got talking and she was telling him about me and my job? With you?"

A lead boot rammed into my solar plexus. "She was telling him about ..."

"Not the ... you know," Amanda lowered her voice and looked around conspiratorially. "But she told him how I was doing this part-time work for you and how I was going to be making a bunch of money in a month or so, and she said he was asking her all these questions. And I thought you should know? You know? Just because?" She shook her head. "That guy is just kind of creepy."

"There's no 'kind of' about it. He is a creep."

"Then why is he on your team?"

"We needed one more player."

"Phew. Well. Anyway? I just thought you should know? Oh, there's Jenny. Gotta go. See ya tomorrow."

She skipped off into the shadows, leaving me to my dark thoughts and the mosquitoes.

I drove home slowly, letting the cares of the day fall from me with each bend in the road, and each toke from the healing evening joint. Rufie rested his paws on the edge of the open shotgun-side window, drinking in the summer scents. By the time I shut off the engine it would be fair to say that I had regained my customary composure.

Naturally, in this trying tournament season, it couldn't last.

As I stepped onto my porch I noticed a shadow on one of the chairs, so I wasn't completely surprised when it spoke and turned out to be Morris. I was actually relieved to find him there, since I felt that his good counsel could help me prepare for the coming fray.

"Nice game today," he began.

I sunk into the chair beside him, shaking my head.

"That's quite a little team you have there," he continued. "I like your surrogate Sammy Sosa. Fun to watch."

I waited for the but. I knew there had to be one. Morris only carpets you with praise so that he can more easily pull the rug out from under you with criticism.

He paused, to allow me to stick my neck out, but I was content to let him do the talking, and confident that he would. After a moment he started up again.

"Whose idea was it to allow mutants to compete in the tournament?"

"They are big."

"They're more than big. They seem to project a kind of Marvel Comics invulnerability. And yet, I understand they came from Prince William?"

"That's right."

"So what idiot let them in?"

"I don't know. And it doesn't matter now. They're here. We're stuck with them."

Morris nodded quietly. "Have you any thoughts on how you might be able to beat them, as it appears more than likely you'll face them again in the final?"

"No. I was hoping you might have a suggestion."

"Perhaps some pot might inspire me."

I knew it. I pulled out the stash and rolled another joint, and for a minute or two we stoked the inner fires of schemery.

"Maybe you should bake some brownies for them," he suggested.

"Yeah. We talked about that. I don't think they'd accept anything from us. DK knows what kind of brownies we make. He used to date Amanda, you know."

"Hmm. Too bad. Some pot might take the edge off those boys."

"They have edge to spare."

We were silent for a few more minutes. I began to fear that this was one of those rare occasions when even Morris couldn't help. A moment later he confirmed this.

"Duggie, my boy, I'm afraid I don't see a way out of this one. I'll let you know if I come up with anything, but, frankly, we may have to accept the unpleasant fact that this year, the good guys aren't going to win. And as for those out-of-town muscle beach bums—as you would say, *possunt quia posse videntur.*"

"They can because they seem to be able to," I translated.

"So it seems."

I slept uneasily that night, harassed by dreams in which strange women kept popping up and pinching me, while terriers nipped at my ankles. Exhausting. Came the dawn, I discovered that Rufie had nested on the covers by my feet, and perhaps his fleas had played a part in the night's entertainment. At any rate, I donned my usual mantle of optimism, chugged a cup of coffee, and drove out to meet with some of the team for breakfast.

Randall, Darren and Photon were in good spirits when I came upon them feasting at the café. They seemed convinced that an easy victory awaited us. I hadn't the heart to tell them of Eduardo's threatened desertion. After all, I reasoned, it might be that Jenny's mystery woman would work the required miracle and motivate our slugger to slug as never before. Stranger things have happened. Especially in Rapidan. But I digress.

I loaded up a plate with bacon, hash browns and donuts and proceeded to fuel the tank. I was so absorbed in the repast that I might have missed the arrival but for the collective gasp at the table. I glanced up. They were all staring out the window with that look men get when a creature from a higher dimension moves near. Their mouths hung open. Their eyes betrayed a hunger no amount of hash browns could satisfy. I looked out the window and choked on my bacon.

Jenny was walking across the parking lot. But it wasn't that. With her was Marilyn Rider, Rapidan's answer to Shakira. She was wearing a form-fitting leopard-skin mini-dress, and let me tell you, her form is the kind that the phrase oo-la-la was coined to describe. Marilyn works at the bar in the Front Royal bowling alley, and many a lad who never dreamed of bowling a strike has dreamed of striking a fire in Marilyn's heart. Because, on top of those curves, or rather, underneath them I guess, technically, she has a famously soft heart for losers.

I swallowed my bacon and began to breath easier. I caught Jenny's eye and gave her the high sign. I never would have thought of Marilyn, but now that she was here, I realized she was the clear choice, the stealth blonde bombshell who could take Eduardo's broken heart and make him forget it had ever been dented. I could hardly wait.

Needless to say, when Marilyn and Jenny left the café to go to the field, they were followed by the entire entourage of gaping men. There's no point in pretending to be immune to the biological imperative. We are but human.

When we got to the field the Sandblasters were doing their warm-up calisthenics. The air rang with their simian grunts. I wondered if they would be impervious to Marilyn.

Jenny jabbed me with her elbow. I snapped to attention and turned just in time to see Eduardo's face when Marilyn walked up to him and introduced herself. I don't know what she said, but you could tell he liked it. And the way she threaded her arm through his and looked up into his eyes.

"What'd I tell you?" whispered Jenny.

"This is great," I said. But a crackle of conscience flickered like static in my head. "I hope he's not too pissed when he finds out it was all a set up."

Jenny nudged me. "Don't worry. Marilyn was happy to come. Apparently word's gotten around about your boy, and she was already looking to meet him. Girls like a big hitter."

"Oh really?" I stiffened. The subject of athletic prowess is a touchy one for those of us whose strengths rest above our shoulders.

Jenny smiled. "Duggie. You know I don't love you for your batting average."

"You don't love me period."

She smiled again. One of those enigmatic ones. "Is that what you think?"

While I was struggling to craft a witty response, she walked away. The game was about to start. I ambled over to the spectator side and noticed that Eduardo and Marilyn were sitting close together, apart from the crowd. So far, so good.

I selected a spot in the shade at the back of the crowd, high enough to see the entire field. I had been observing the proceedings for a few minutes, when a grating voice began to register on the mental scanner. There was something familiar about it. And not in a good way. I peered over the heads of the crowd and caught sight of a woman in a red and white striped shirt and a navy skirt. Her hair was shellacked like a biker's helmet. I recognized her as the newspaper woman whom I'd overheard Shipley sucking up to. She was carrying a little tape recorder with a microphone, and she was followed by a lackey with an assortment of cameras hung around his neck.

I wondered if Shipley realized that his team was about to get hammered by the Sandblasters. Perhaps he hadn't paid any attention to the other games. If he had invited the media here to witness the Swans' triumph, he was in for a surprise. I had to smile. No doubt even Shipley would appreciate the irony.

The game began with the Sandblasters at bat. They scored two runs. The Swans went three up, three down. This set the pattern for the rest of the game. By the seventh inning the Sandblasters were up 14 to nothing and Shipley was fuming. I could have told him not to bother. Sometimes, fate kicks you in the shins. The only thing to do is rub the spot until it stops hurting and move on. As Livy noted, *vae victus*— it's tough to be a loser.

Shipley, apparently, hadn't absorbed the teachings of the Romans. His loss. Also, the Swans. But they, at least, had no illusions of victory before the debacle started. There was one brief shining moment, when Babe snagged a pop fly and threw it to third to nail the base runner for a double play that ended the eighth inning. But, it wasn't enough to remove the sting of defeat.

When it was over, the Sandblasters did their disappearing act, and Shipley ranted into the reporter's microphone for a while. I heard him using the terms "fair play" and "level playing field" and had to laugh. But then, while the Moonlighters were getting warmed up, I detected a shift in the tone of rant and glanced over. Shipley's purple face was looming over Jenny, and you could tell he was venting freely. I didn't have to hear the words to know that he was the sort of twerp who needed to assign blame for every loss, and that, in this case, Jenny was the target of choice. I would have gone over and defended her, but I knew she didn't need my help.

Suddenly, her voice rose above the rest. "That's it, you scumbag! I quit."

"You can't quit. You're fired!" shrieked Shipley.

"Too late! I already quit!"

"You'll never work in this town again!"

"Hah! Get over yourself! This isn't your town, and it never will be!"

The crowd, which had been following this exchange, burst into cheers and applause at this point. I had never loved Jenny more.

But my moment of glowing pride was cut short by a tug at my sleeve. "Come on, Duggie. We got a game to play," said Witty.

I trotted over to field, my spirits high even though I was not, at that moment, technically, stoned. My plan was to snag a few tokes in the outfield during the seventh inning stretch if, as I expected, we had the game well in hand by then.

As it transpired, I was able to achieve lift-off by the end of the fifth, thanks to the effect of Marilyn's presence on Eduardo's will to win. He socked the first pitch that came his way into the unmowed regions of the outfield, then trotted leisurely round the bases, doffing his cap to Marilyn as he touched home. And, it must be said, that even as she inspired our star player to new heights, she dazzled the Firemen to such an extent that they dropped balls that they normally could have fielded with their eyes closed. In fact, they might have done better blindfolded. Well, that's probably not true. In all honesty, the Moonlighters might have won without her, and it's possible that a moral nitpicker might find fault with the tactic, but let's not kid ourselves. Those Dallas cheerleaders aren't on the sidelines solely to distract the crowd. Wiles and stratagems are an integral part of any sporting event worth watching. And Marilyn was an eyeful.

Also, in our defense, I must report that we had to play the entire game shorthanded, due to the mysterious non-appearance of Kevin. Such is my contempt for the weasel that I confess I only noticed he was missing when Roy Spooner connected with one of Darren's less erratic pitches, and the ball sailed high and deep into left field which, I suddenly noticed, was completely devoid of outfielders. When we came in at the end of the inning I learned that Kevin had told someone he wouldn't be coming today because he had a stomach ache. Funny he hadn't told me.

CHAPTER 8

dum vita est spes est
While there's life, there's hope.

I was sitting on the tailgate of my truck, watching Rufie snapping at the fireflies which were beginning to shimmy out of the tall grass in the unmowed portions of the outfield. I was halfway through the reefer I had brought along to soothe the nerves which inevitably frayed during the heat of a taxing athletic contest. Not that it was all that taxing, of course. I mean, we beat the Firemen, 5-2, and no one suffered a loss of face during the proceedings. But, there was no getting away from the lurking dread. In the final game tomorrow, the Sandblasters loomed like one of those Midwestern tornadoes on the horizon. You might be able to survive the encounter if you get down to the basement and hang on tight to the plumbing, but you know there's no way you're not going to lose a lot. I was on the verge of being depressed. Thus the healing joint.

"Is this the best place to do that?"

I jumped up coughing and turned to see Morris, who had materialized out of thin air the way he does. "You scared me."

"You should be scared."

I frowned. Was the man trying to bring me down? "Of the Sandblasters? Of course I'm scared. They're like skinheads with bats."

"I wasn't referring to them, though they do project a kind of *Terminator* machismo."

"If by that you mean they're heartless bastards, then, yes, I agree. Arnold would welcome them as brothers."

I took a long drag on the joint and offered it to Morris, who sucked at it reflectively. I tried in vain to regain my calm, but his earlier remark had fanned the pilot light of paranoia that burns constantly inside every pothead.

"What do you think I should be scared of?"

Morris glanced around briefly before he replied, *sotto voce*, "The Sheriff."

"Quayle?" I scoffed. This dickhead sheriff had been beating the bushes for years trying to flush out the resident moonshiners, pot farmers and harmless hippies. We all loathed him as a result, and worked together to foil his tiresome vendetta. His motivation, everyone knew, was based on his belief that a big bust of some sort would give him a foothold on the career ladder of crime prevention. His upward mobility had so far been hampered by the drag of his idiot son's misdemeanors, which ranged from simple vandalism to car theft. Some of the more sociology-minded among us viewed Kevin's petty crime spree as a cry for help. The rest of us simply reveled in the pure ironic beauty of it.

"Even a blind pig finds a nut now and then," Morris said.

"You mean Quayle? What makes you think he's looking?"

"Doesn't it strike you as suspicious that the sheriff's n'ere do well son suddenly takes an interest in softball at the very time that a certain crop is nearing harvest?"

"Shhh," I hissed. I peered into the darkness surrounding us.

"My point exactly. I noticed he wasn't among those present during today's game. Do you have any idea where he was?"

"No. I've got more important things to worry about."

Morris shook his head. "Don't underestimate the little twerp. That's all I'll say."

"Fine. I'll keep an eye on him next time he shows up."

Morris went off into the night, and I tried to recapture the mellow mood that had come upon me before his intrusion. It wasn't that easy. I found myself wondering if a blind pig would have had better success. And why blind necessarily? Surely a blindfold would be sufficient to hamper a porker? I was musing along these lines when a distinctly unporcine aroma caught my attention—a hint of roses and similar blossoms, along with a smidgeon of possibly Dr. Pepper. I opened my eyes, which I had shut to aid my concentration, and discovered that Phoebe had joined me, her smile beaming like a flashlight.

"Hey you," she said. "I thought I might find you out here under the stars."

I smirked. It would have taken a better man than I not to be soothed by this girl's open enthusiasm for my company. "Hello. Would you like some of this?" I offered her the joint but she merely smiled and shook her head.

"No thanks. It makes me too confused, and I'm not as smart as you are to begin with."

"Oh, I'm sure that's not true," I said, though, honestly, I have no idea how she did in school. I mean, I barely know the girl. But, her obvious attraction to me demonstrates a degree of intelligence that not every member of her gender exhibits. So I was inclined to give her the benefit of the doubt.

She slid next to me on the tailgate in a friendly way, rubbing her shoulder against my side. "You know Duggie, I was thinking about your game tomorrow."

"And?"

"And I was thinking you should have cheerleaders."

"Really?"

"Yeah. It would be good for the team spirit."

"You think so? They don't usually have cheerleaders for softball."

"I know. If they did maybe people wouldn't think it was so boring. There would at least be something to watch while you're waiting for something to happen. What do you think?"

"Well," I inhaled and held it for a while, then coughed a bit and said, " I guess it couldn't hurt. But we can't go out and hire some cheerleaders before tomorrow."

"You don't have to." She grinned at me. "Just leave it to me." Then she leaned closer and kissed me full on the lips. I don't recall exactly what I did then, beyond a kind of mild recoil to get clear of her. But I do remember what she did next, which was to put her hand on my thigh and give a squeeze as she whispered, "I'll take care of you, Duggie."

Then she slipped off the truck and vanished with a giggle. I don't know how long I would have remained there in a state somewhere between confusion and arousal, but the question became moot when Jenny abruptly materialized before me looking none too happy.

"So. That's what you've been doing. Here I was worrying about you, looking all over for you, imagining you getting depressed about tomorrow, and all the time you've been out here making out with your little Latin groupie."

I sat up straighter, though in doing so noticed that I was a lot more stoned than I'd realized. "We weren't making out."

"Uh hunh. I don't care what you call it, Duggie. I know what I saw."

"For your information, Phoebe came to tell me that she's going to get cheerleaders for us."

"What do you mean, cheerleaders?"

"I mean, you know, pom poms, short skirts, bouncing . . . you know . . . cheerleaders."

Jenny snorted softly. "Uh hunh. Well, I'm sure that'll be a big help."

"Hey. She's just a kid. It can't hurt."

Jenny tapped her foot on the gravel. "I suppose not. But you're going to need more than . . . bouncing to beat those bastards."

"I know that. Do you have any ideas?"

She glared at me for a few seconds more before she seemed to turn a page. Then she shook herself and said, "Okay. Here's what I'm offering. It's not as exciting as cheerleaders, but," she frowned and seemed to hesitate before she continued. "Okay. You know Shitley fired me? And the Swans are history. So, I'm a free agent. And I know you've got Darren, but I was thinking you might like to have me and Babe back on the team."

My jaw dropped and the stars flickered. "You mean it?"

"I wouldn't say it if I didn't mean it."

"That would be . . . that would be . . . fantastic!"

"Are you sure? You don't think Darren will be pissed?"

"I doubt it. Did you see when he got hit by one of those Sandblaster line drives? He was ready to quit right then. I had to persuade him to stay on by telling him it was okay to aim right at them."

"You told him to aim right at them?"

I shrugged. "He only hit a couple of them. Darren's aim isn't his strong suit."

Jenny nodded. "True."

"But I bet he'd be happy to be let off the hook for tomorrow. I can put him out in the outfield to take Kevin's place."

"Yeah. What happened there? I noticed you were playing down a man."

"Would you call him a man?"

Jenny grinned, but it didn't last long. "I'm glad he's gone anyway. I don't trust that little rat." She hesitated, then said, "It's not gonna be easy tomorrow."

"Yeah, I know. It could be pretty bleak."

"But at least we'll have cheerleaders." She smiled as she said this, and of course, then I didn't care how bleak the future looked, as long as Jenny was on my team.

A short while later Jenny and I were enjoying the convivial atmosphere in the Toad, where, despite the impending ordeal, most of the Moonlighters were carousing with a carefree abandon that did your heart good to see. So buoyant were my spirits that I had just slipped my hand under the table to squeeze Jenny's thigh, in hopes I could get away with it under the banner of general carousal, when the door banged open and all the joy went out of the room as DK came into it.

I wish I could report that at this moment we all carried on as if he weren't there. Instead we all stared at him, and the two requisite goons flanking him, as if they were the Four Horsemen of the Apocalypse making up in bulk what they lacked in numbers. Everyone in the room stopped talking, and you could have heard a pin drop, but for the fact that the jukebox was still playing—that Dylan song, "Gotta Serve Somebody," droned like a battle hymn in the background.

A grin slithered across DK's wide jaw.

"So this is where y'all hide out," he drawled, rotating his big head to take in the room. "What a dump," he sniffed. Then he glanced at his sidekicks. "Might as well get a beer, long as we're here."

The loathsome trio lumbered to the bar. No one else spoke. It was like we were in one of those old westerns where the baddie shows up, and you can feel the brawl scene looming in the ozone. No one wanted to spark it off.

Harold, the bartender, pulled the drafts and set them before DK, Brick and the other guy I didn't know. Then DK turned and looked around the room until he caught my eye. My nails must have dug into Jenny's thigh, because she punched my shoulder and pulled away. DK smirked. "Hey you. It's Duggie, right?"

I nodded.

"You the captain of that sorry ass team?"

"What sorry ass team?"

DK chuckled. "Well I guess you're right. They's more 'n one out here ain't there?" He smirked at his pals as he said this, and they provided backup smirks. The Smirkettes. I could have said this out loud, but I'm not suicidal.

"Them Moon guys. You their captain?"

I sat up straighter and looked him in the eyes, small and beady as they were. "I'm the captain."

"Well good. Cause I want to offer you a deal. You're gonna lose tomorrow. You know it. I know it. Everybody in this room knows it." He paused for a second. "So, me and the boys was thinking it would save everybody a lot of time and trouble if we just picked up the trophy tonight and call off the slaughter tomorrow." He shrugged. "We figure, you guys've been humiliated enough. We don't need to stomp you twice. Plus, some of the boys have other things they'd like to do tomorrow, it bein' the Fourth of July an all. You know, we came out here thinking it might be some competition. But, let's face it. It's like scuba diving in the baby pool. No fun. So what do you say?"

I stood up. I wanted to make sure that everyone heard me loud and clear when I told him to shove it. But, as it turned out, I never got the chance, because, before I opened my mouth, a bull charged across the room and butted DK head first, knocking him to the floor. In the instant before the rest of the room exploded into mayhem, I realized that the bull was actually Photon, his face red with fury, his fists pounding like piledrivers. He continued pummeling DK while Brick and the other guy tried to pull him off, their efforts hampered by the crowd of allies kicking, punching, and, I regret to say, in some cases biting them. How long this lasted I couldn't tell you, as my head connected with something sharp and hard early on, and I kind of lost track of the proceedings. But, when the last beer bottle had crashed to the floor, and DK and his evil twins had exited stage left, the mood in the room was far from calm.

"Man, I'd like to kill those sons' of bitches," said Randall, brushing broken glass off his chest.

A mutter of agreement rose in the room.

Then Witty stood up and said, "Yeah, well, talk's cheap. If we could talk those guys to death, we could just set Duggie on 'em. But if we want to beat 'em tomorrow we're gonna have to come up with something else."

I looked over at Jenny, and I could see by her expression that she agreed. I considered mentioning the cheerleaders, but decided against it. Even I knew that cheerleaders alone wouldn't be enough to turn the odds in our favor. But, as I looked around at the room at Photon and Randall and Babe and all the rest of them, I wondered if maybe we had a few more wild cards hidden in our hand.

"Okay. You're right," I said. "But I know this: we may not be as big as those guys, or as tough, or as mean, or even as good at playing ball. But we're definitely smarter. There's got to be a way we can beat 'em. This is Rapidan. This is our tournament, and we can't let a bunch of guys from Prince William come in and steal it from us."

Photon banged his fist on a table. "All in favor say aye."

A few voices mumbled "aye."

Photon banged his fist harder. "I can't hear you."

"Aye!" came the response, louder this time.

"Say it like you mean it!"

"AYE!"

Photon smiled at me. "You got a plan, right?" he said in a quiet voice.

I grimaced. "Working on it," I mumbled.

For the truth was, in spite of my brave words, I had no idea how we could level the playing field. Later, as we filed out of the Toad, I beckoned Witt and Eric and Jenny to come back to my place for a strategy session. I figured if we got high together we had a better chance of stumbling onto an inspiration.

I hadn't noticed that Amanda was more or less affixed to Eric at this point, and following her like a lesser moon was Mindy, the pet sitter. This in itself wouldn't have bothered me, but I remembered Amanda's warning about Kevin's interest in this girl, and I suddenly wondered where Kevin had been all this time. I saw no signs of weasel about the girl as she traipsed into my house, but I can't deny it made me uneasy. I decided to clear the air before filling it with pot smoke.

"Hey Mindy, I heard Kevin was hitting on you. Have you seen him lately? Do you know why he wasn't at the game today?"

Mindy turned her baby doll eyes at me. "Gosh, Duggie. I didn't know you cared."

I floundered. "I don't. I mean, I do. I mean, it's not ..." I looked at Jenny for help.

She rolled her eyes and turned to Mindy. "Duggie's worried that Kevin's going to narc him out to his dad."

Mindy's wide eyes grew wider. "Oooh. Hah. Of course." She giggled. "Don't worry, Duggie," she said and slapped my shoulder in a girlish way that caused Jenny to reroll her eyes. "I would never rat on you. I'm not as dumb as I look."

"Good to know," I said. But, try as I might to take comfort in her assurance, I felt that, even if this child were not as dumb as she looked, she could still be plenty dumb enough to have let slip a remark that would tip off a rodent like Kevin. Still, as I got the trusty shoebox and began rolling spliffs, I reminded myself that no good comes of worrying about the future. For the moment, the urgent concern was to devise a surefire plan to deliver defeat to our enemies.

But, after we had been studying the problem for a while, Witt shook his head and said, "I don't know, Duggie. I don't see any way we can nuke these guys."

"What have we got that they don't have?" asked Jenny.

"Good looks won't win you the ball game," said Eric.

Mindy pursed her lips and said, "Maybe you don't have to win so much if you can make them lose."

Everyone turned on her at this seeming witless remark, and I was on the verge of saying something pithy, when Amanda piped up. "That's right. You guys don't have to outplay them. You just have to make them lose it."

"Well, yeah," I began scornfully.

"No, wait," Jenny interrupted. She turned to Mindy and said, "Do you have an idea?"

"Well, my brother Andrew? He's got these guys he plays paintball with—the Scurvy Pirates? They go out in the woods and shoot at each other all the time. I bet they'd be happy to go sniper on the Sandblasters."

"Hot damn!" Witty slapped his thigh. "That's the best idea I've heard all day."

I had to agree. Now that she'd said it, I realized I'd been overlooking a whole fruitful sector of warcraft. Guerilla tactics.

The tried and tested method of underdogs the world over. Suddenly my mind was aflame with ideas.

"That's great! Do you think you can get them lined up before tomorrow?"

"I'll call him now," Mindy said, and scampered from the room.

"She's right, you know," Eric said. "But if you're going to booby trap the field, you'll have to be careful you don't trip up your own team."

"Right. We don't need to go overboard. But if we can just throw them off, make them slip up here and there, we'll have a chance," I said.

We continued plotting along these lines, and by the time the session adjourned we had a fully sketched hazy grab bag of tricks, any one of which might backfire. But, at least we weren't going into the game empty-handed. Half-cocked maybe, but that's better than the other thing.

Jenny gave me a little hug as she left. "Sleep tight slugger," she said. "Tomorrow's going to be a big day."

I was nodding off in a reasonably close approximation of peace when the phone began ringing. I ignored it at first, figuring I had just talked with everyone I needed to talk to, and anyone calling at one in the morning was probably drunk or otherwise confused. But the phone didn't stop even after I flipped it up and snapped it closed without a word. The ringing resumed seconds later and continued until finally, fighting the urge to throw it out the window, I lifted it to my ear and immediately regretted it.

"What is wrong with you? Are you so stoned you can't pick up the phone? Or were you passed out from celebrating your victory? I've been standing here for ten minutes! I was beginning to think you'd flushed your phone again."

This taunt went too far and I found voice at last. "Do you know what time it is?" I began coolly.

"You're damn right I do! It's time for you to wake up and smell the disaster! Are you aware that Eduardo is considering defecting to Shitley? And that the Post's food critic came tonight and was all set to write the review of a lifetime until one of the waiters mentioned that the chef might be moving across the street?"

My mouth was open, but the witty rebuttal I had mapped out had fizzled into nothingness under this barrage. "Why would Eduardo leave now?"

"Because, you fool, Shitley has offered him a pile of gold, and, now that you've managed to completely jinx the Rosalie aspect of the picture, he doesn't see any reason why he should stay on here."

"Did he already quit?"

"No. But tonight he said he was thinking about it. Shitley wants him to start tomorrow."

"But he can't do that. We have a game tomorrow."

"Yeah. Well. About that? Who are you kidding? Nobody's going to beat those guys." She paused and if I hadn't been so rattled by her remarks I might have tried to say something at this point, but the moment passed and she was off and ranting again. "If you want to know the truth, I think Eduardo doesn't want to lose to those Sandmen again in front of his new girlfriend. Boy, she's a hot tamale. It's too bad, because I think she's got Eduardo's mojo all revved up, and he wants to show off for her, but he's no fool. Those sand guys are out of our league."

"Yes. That's true. DK and his crew should never have been allowed in the tournament. I think we can all agree on this. However, all is not lost. I have a plan."

"Hah! That's all we need. I'm about to be run out of business by that snake Shitley, but my worries are over because you have a plan?"

I drew myself up. I was used to the scorn of this woman. These pushy big sisters never know when to quit. "I'm assuming you woke me from a sound sleep because you wanted my help," I said.

"I don't know why I called you. As if you could fix anything."

I reminded myself that this woman had given me a job and, when we were children, had often shared her last Oreo with me. I could overlook her insults.

"Glory, I know you don't have much faith in me. But I'll talk to Eduardo in the morning. I'll get Jenny to talk to him. We'll fix it. Don't worry."

A loud sigh echoed through the phone line. "Fine. I guess even you can't make things any worse."

She hung up. I sat there for a while debating whether or not to call Jenny and get her advice. Then I thought better of it. Let her get a good night's sleep first.

CHAPTER 9

fortes fortuna iuvat
Fortune favors the brave.

A merry slip of sunshine played upon my face in the morning, and the glowing warmth woke me in an unusually good mood, which lasted a full five minutes before I remembered the stern work ahead. A glance at the clock told me it was only four hours till game time. I couldn't afford to wait until a civilized hour to call Jenny.

"This better be good," she mumbled, when she answered on the sixth ring.

"Well, I don't think 'good' is the most accurate descriptor," I began, but that's as far as I got.

"Duggie? What's up? Have the sand bastards forfeited?"

"Nice thought. But, no. I'm afraid it's not as good as that." I proceeded to fill her in on the recent developments in the Eduardo scenario, and she quickly grasped the essentials.

"Okay, okay. We can manage this. I'll just have a word with Marilyn. I'm sure she can explain the situation to Eduardo in terms he can understand."

The vulture of anxiety perched on my shoulders lifted off and disappeared. "You mean?"

"Sure. At this point, whatever Marilyn wants, Marilyn gets. And I know Eduardo wants her to be happy. So. Consider it done."

"That's great. But, we haven't got much time."

"So hang up. I'm on it."

I hung up and thought about what Horace said: *nil desperandum*. Never say die. So true.

By the time I had eaten a nourishing breakfast and suited up for the final showdown, however, a nagging shadow of doubt had returned, as if that vulture had circled back to see if the coast was clear.

It was all well and good that the Eduardo angle was under control, but the big picture still looked murky. Plus, when I stepped out on the porch the humidity slapped me like a wet towel. I hadn't noticed it so much inside. I guess I must have thought it was just residual steam from my shower. But outside the air had the feel of a clambake, from the clam's perspective. Virginia in July. It's not for the faint of heart.

I opened the truck door for Rufie, he jumped inside, and off we went. The ride down the mountain had that peaceful, calm-before-the-storm kind of feeling. Shafts of golden light slanted down through the trees, casting bright bars across the road. The scent of honeysuckle and wild roses blew in the window where Rufie had his head stuck out, his ears flapping like towels on a laundry line. He, at least, appeared to be enjoying the moment. I confess, my usual *que sera, sera* attitude was not up to speed. For all my brave talk in front of the troops, I had a bad feeling about this day.

When I got to the field, though, I put on my reddish badge of courage, though I wished I could inhale some of my greenish smoke instead. If we were going to get annihilated, I would prefer to be stoned when it happened. But I knew I couldn't pretend to lead the troops if I got hammered, so I affixed the grin and jogged to the outfield to warm up.

As I went past the stands I noticed an unusually glittery section, and when one patch of it detached itself from the rest and trotted toward me, I saw that it was, in fact, Phoebe, the star-struck Latinista.

"Hi, Duggie!" she said, waving a pompom. "What do you think?" She twirled to give me the 360-degree view of her cheerleading outfit, and, I have to say, what there was of it was certainly eye-catching, and what there wasn't, so to speak, was even more so. The bare-midriff portion seemed to extend well below where mids usually riff, and, in consequence, the eye was drawn, hypnotically it seemed, to the jewel dangling from her navel, which, for the record, was an innie.

"It's nice," I said, trying unsuccessfully not to stare at the tight satin shorts that didn't come close to covering her small, yet perfectly proportioned, butt.

She kicked up her heels, literally her thigh-high blue leather boots, and giggled. "Wait till you see our routines. Those guys aren't going to be watching the ball if we have anything to do with it."

"Great," I said, with a dazed smile. For, truth be told, I wasn't sure the Moonlighters would be exactly immune to the cheerleaders' charms. I began to wonder if the whole thing might backfire. But, as I watched Phoebe scamper back to her cheer mates, I felt that it was too late to put the stopper back in the bottle of mischief. Madness was already in the air, tangible as ragweed and far, far more potent.

I joined the team in desultory warm up. Sweat was already dripping off Eduardo's face, and in Photon's eyes the melt-down warning light was already pulsating. In the trees that ringed the ball park the shrill buzz of cicadas whined like an alien force field. You got the feeling that it wouldn't take much to light this powder keg. Only Jenny and Babe seemed to be feeling enthusiasm of the sort described by Vince Lombardi as an essential element in any winning strategy.

I swallowed a gnat moodily and thwocked my ball against my glove, frowning at the colorless sky above. It wasn't exactly cloudy. But it was a far cry from blue. It had a kind of empty, psychotic look, as if it hadn't decided yet whether to slash us to ribbons with lightning and cannon thunder or whether to float off and inflict itself on some other unsuspecting village.

Weather. Pah.

A shrill whistle blast announced an end to the pre-game ritual. I saw the Sandblasters lined up at their bench, in pre-gloat mode. The Moonlighters were huddled like shipwreck victims drawing straws to see who gets eaten first. I walked over to join them.

"Well, Duggie? Got any last words of advice?" said Witty.

I looked around at my team—Witty, Photon, Randall, Eduardo, Rosalie, Babe, Darren and Jenny—and I felt a surge of pride that nearly choked me up. I tried to think of some inspiring slogan, some verbal charm that would ward off the slaughter I knew in my heart was coming. I didn't look up at the sky. It was not on our side this dank day. I stubbed my toe in the dirt and closed my eyes and it came to me. "Rule number one," I said.

They looked at me for a second, and then Jenny grinned. "Right," she said, nodding. "It's rule number one. That's the only one we play by."

Everyone but Rosalie and Eduardo nodded.

"What is rule number one?" asked Rosalie.

The rest of us whispered it together. "There are no rules."

Eduardo grinned. "Hokay," he said.

I put my hand in to the middle of the huddle and everyone else added theirs to mine. "Okay, it's gonna be rough. And it might get weird too. But remember, weird is our strong suit. So we gotta play it. Got it?"

"Got it!" they all whispered.

We broke the huddle and lined up for the coin toss.

No sooner had DK won the toss, however, than his sneer of victory grew uglier as he caught sight of Jenny heading for the mound.

"Hey! What's she doing on your team?" he said.

I turned to him and replied, "She's our pitcher."

His frown hardened. "She can't be on your team. She was with that other bunch of losers. The ducks."

I allowed a trace of amusement into my cool demeanor. "Perhaps you're referring to the Swans? Yes. We loaned Jenny to the Swans for the preliminary rounds of the tournament, but now that we're in the final, she is naturally back with us."

"You can't do that."

"Oh, but we can. And we have. *Praesto et persto*. Get over it."

DK goggled at me as if he were one brain cell away from strangling me, but, as luck would have it, that cell held, and the moment passed. He glared for about another half a minute, and I could tell he was dying to know what I had said, but was damned if he was going to ask for a translation. This is one of the beautiful things about Latin. It confounds your enemies and leaves them no retort.

Eventually DK seemed to sense that he had lost the upper hand. Through clenched teeth he grumbled, "Fine. Let's get this over with."

He stomped back to the bench and we could hear him venting furiously to his fellow goons.

Then Art blew his horn and yelled "play ball!" and we all spat on our hands, figuratively speaking in most cases, and got down to work.

And, for the first few pitches, the breath of hope stirred in our collective chests. But, on the sixth pitch, Brick Nunley connected with a report that set all the dogs howling. The ball sailed deep into left field, where Darren was occupying the space left by the deserter Kevin. I say occupying since that's a more accurate term than playing when describing Darren's fielding skills. Sadly, Darren's wizardry in pitching represents the full extent of his softball skills. In his defense, he made an effort to catch the ball. But a closer analysis of his technique revealed that his primary goal was self-preservation. He didn't want to get hit in the head by the ball, he explained later, and if indeed that was his objective, then it should be noted that he succeeded. But, by the time the ball was recovered from the knee-high grass, Nunley was well on his way to third base, and we managed to hold him there only by, well, holding him there. Eduardo latched onto his ankles and refused to let go in spite of Nunley's vigorous efforts to kick himself free.

When the dust settled, you could see the Sandblasters mumbling among themselves, as if weighing this new trick in the play book. They didn't care for it much, but I guessed they weren't going to use elocution to make their point.

And, when DK himself came up to bat next, he left no doubt that he had gotten the message about Rapidan rules.

He missed the first two pitches, and Jenny gave him nothing to hit on the following two. But then he crouched down and nailed the fifth pitch, sending a line drive screaming past me and out to where Photon was pacing like an attack dog on a short chain. He lunged at the ball and got it on the first hop, but DK was streaking toward second, and when he got there he didn't even pause. He drove his fists into Randall and sent him sprawling while he continued pounding to third. There, Eduardo very alertly tripped him and that put an end to that. But Nunley had already scored.

The rest of their batting order proceeded to chip and bang away at Jenny's pitches, and I could see she was feeling frustrated. We managed to get two outs by wrestling the runners to the ground between bases. But we weren't having any luck stopping them from hitting. I was wondering if we might not be better off with wild man Darren when Jenny took action.

At first I thought she was just stretching. But then a gasp arose from the stands, and I looked back and nearly swallowed my tongue. Jenny had taken off her shirt and was going through her wind-up motion wearing only a hot pink sports bra above her shorts.

Her sacrifice was not in vain. The gorilla at bat swung mightily, but you could tell he wasn't watching the ball all the way to the plate as the best coaches advise. Within a minute he had struck out, and our cheerleaders finally had something to shout about.

Jenny put her shirt back on when the team came in for our at bat, but I took her aside and asked if perhaps she would consider applying the same method when her turn came at the plate. She smiled coyly and said she wouldn't rule it out.

Unfortunately I didn't get a chance to find out whether Jenny would take my advice during that inning, because the first two up, Darren and Witty, struck out in such a convincing manner that when Photon stepped up to the plate the rest of us were already reaching for our gloves. Photon was already glowing with a thermal warmth that led those who knew him to familiarize themselves with retreat routes.

Wrath alone can never guarantee success, however, and Photon's first two swings met only with air. Then he took a step back from the plate, wiggled his ass defiantly, and stepped back for the next pitch. It was a high slider that dipped just before it reached him, but Photon swung smoothly and knocked it high into center field, where it was picked off easily, thus ending the first inning. We were only down by one run, and, considering, we took that as a good sign.

Sadly, the Sandblasters seemed to have discovered some antidote to Jenny's pink bra, and they quickly got two men on base before we managed to get the next batter out at first. Then DK came to the plate, his evil grin shining like a roadside flare at a car crash—nothing good could come of this. I guess Jenny must have had the same thought, because she hit him on the ass with the next pitch, and you can't really do that unless you're trying. I understood her reasoning. She figured it was worth letting the bases get loaded in the hope that the next batter might be easier to dispatch. With any ordinary team of mortals, that strategy would apply.

But, the Sandblasters, as I believe I mentioned earlier, were mutant dolts from one of the lower-rent circles of hell, and they had no shortage of sledgehammer hitters. One of these drones stepped up to the plate next, and I looked over to see how Jenny responded, but she was cool as can be and didn't let on that she had been hoping for something in a medium.

The guy smacked a screamer into center field, and they scored two runs on it, but at least we got him out when he tried to get to second. Could have been worse, I suppose.

Somehow we got the third out before they scored again, so by the time we came up to bat we were only down by three. Now if only we could find a way to score.

Witty came over to me on the sidelines and whispered. "Hey. When are you going to set the pirates on 'em? We can't just let 'em run up the score on us. We'll never catch up."

I nodded. He raised a good point. However as the fellow said, *tempus anima rei*. Which, for those of you who sold your Latin texts on eBay, means something like "time is the soul of things," or as they say in comedy, timing is everything. I didn't want to unleash the pirates too soon. The idea was to let the sense of chaos build in the Sandblasters' unconscious, or Jungian collective mind, where it would cloud their judgment and play havoc with their reflexes.

That was the plan, anyway. For the time being, we had to hang on and do it the hard way.

Which, for the ensuing several innings we did. Through sheer dogged grit and some creative defensive maneuvers that would have raised eyebrows on a rugby field, we held the Sandblasters to a mere ten run lead by the middle of the seventh inning. I gathered the team together during the stretch break and told them to be alert to opportunities in the next at bat, and then I signaled Mindy's brother.

As luck would have it, our first batter up was Rosalie. She looked fetching as could be in her tight white T-shirt and short shorts, but there was no getting away from the fact that she was the weakest link in our chain. During her first at bat the balls had gone by her so quickly she hadn't even gotten off a swing. She had tripped back to the bench muttering French oaths.

This time, she frowned at the pitcher as she stepped up to the plate, as if she wanted him to understand that she considered him rude. I could have told her this was like pouring gasoline on a burning tire. I pursed the lips instead and waited to see what effect the pirates might have on the play of events.

The first seconds of the pitcher's wind-up offered little hope of change. But then there was a tiny whiz and a distinct "splat" just as the pitcher was rotating to hurl the ball, and the distraction, minor though it seemed from where I watched, seemed to have made a much larger impression on the mound. The pitch, which had at first looked like it would be an untouchable missile, slipped out of the pitcher's hand with a slower looping trajectory, and Rosalie watched it the way a small, very stylish, falcon might watch a fat pigeon that sailed across its path during the lunch hour.

She swung and caught the edge of the ball just enough to make it slither sideways off the bat. She dropped the bat and ran like a gazelle for first base while the catcher scrabbled in the dust to retrieve the ball. By the time he had it under control Rosalie was on base, and the crowd went wild.

Babe was up next, and a woman more unlike Rosalie would be hard to find. She lumbered to the plate and crouched with the bat cocked above her shoulder glaring at the mound. The first pitch was fast and low, but Babe was locked on target and knocked it sailing high into center field. I watched it descend tensely, knowing that, under ordinary circumstances, such a fly ball would be easy pickings for any competent outfielder. Everything depended on a pirate strike.

As the ball dropped closer to the centerfielder's glove, I held my breath, hoping for a precision offensive. And then, just as the ball was an arm's length from his glove, the center fielder hopped on one foot and yelled "Hey!" while the ball bounced harmlessly into the tall grass. Babe thundered past first and secured a place at second before the ball was thrown to the infield. The center fielder was examining his leg, but there didn't appear to be a blotch of paint. I was puzzled by this. I looked over at Mindy, waving her pompoms proudly at the sidelines, and considered asking her what sort of paint the pirates used, but there was no time. I was up.

I strolled to the plate and assumed a stance that I hoped would convey a carefree confidence I did not, at that moment, feel. But, I was somewhat buoyed by the fact that we had two runners on base. My confidence, feigned as it might be, faded when the first ball streaked by me doing about 120 mph. I may be deluded about my abilities, but even I knew there was no way I could hit a pitch like that. I peered into the woods at the edge of the field, and thought I detected a gleam of metal. Hope renewed, I put my trust in the pirates, and, on the next pitch, my faith was rewarded. As the pitcher's arm came up to release the ball there was another one of those faint whizzing sounds, and just as he let go a tiny popping sound was followed by a loud "Hey!" from the mound. I didn't care. I was totally focused on the ball and socked it toward left field while the pitcher clutched his elbow and glared in the direction of the woods. When I looked up from first base, I saw he had called DK over, and the two of them conferred for a couple of minutes, their whispering reminiscent of the way a couple of yellow jackets sound when they get trapped in a soda can. Not happy.

We, on the other hand, were jubilant. We had the bases loaded for the first time in the game, and you could almost smell the euphoria. Randall was up next, and he was one of our best hitters. He wasn't intimidated by the Sandblasters, having played in some tough Little League divisions in his youth. Also, by this time the pitcher was definitely spooked. He kept glancing over his shoulder and jerking his head around as if he were trying to pick off someone stealing a base. As if. But, you never know. When he finally threw a pitch Randall's way, it wasn't the usual smoldering ball of fire, and Randall swung with a relaxed grace that made it look easy and hit a bouncing line drive that hopped over the short stop's glove and continued on into the deep grass of center field.

Rosalie and Babe both scored, while I made it to second, and Randall arrived comfortably on first. The fans were screaming.

And then a silence fell as Eduardo came up to bat.

CHAPTER 10

una salus victis nullam sperare salutem
The one safety for the vanquished is to abandon hope for safety.

When I say silence, perhaps it would be more accurate to report that the crowd fell silent. But, you've probably heard the one about nature abhorring a vacuum? Sure enough, when the hush fell on the crowd as Eduardo stepped to the plate, there was a rumble of thunder like a distant avalanche, ominous as dammit. Shakespeare couldn't have asked for a more chilling portent.

Eduardo didn't appear to notice, even though a shadow fell across the field and a breeze kicked up out of nowhere. The tall grass in the deep outfield was swaying like a restless hula girl, and there was that kind of what's it in the air—you know? You could feel the ozone building up, like when you're rubbing your feet on the carpet so you can annoy your little sister with a touch of static.

The air had taken on that flat yellow color that means no good, and in the next few minutes everything seemed to go in slow motion.

The pitcher drew himself together, holding the ball right under his chin, which was tucked low. His cap was pulled down, hiding his face.

Another, louder, cannonade of thunder shook the clouds. A small child in the crowd called for his mother. I knew how he felt.

Eduardo ignored the dust swirling at his feet. A crackle of lightning ripped through the clouds above. The pitcher went into his windup. The ball flew toward the plate. Eduardo uncoiled his torso and cracked the ball so hard his bat broke, and he took off for first base while the ball soared into center field. As the ball went up, the rain came down.

Another jolt of lightning tore through the sky, and the fielder, looking up into the rain, bobbled the catch. Meanwhile, I scored, and Randall was rounding second. The rain was coming down as if we were in a Bollywood musical, but Randall kept running. The Sandblasters were yelling at each other, or maybe at us. Randall didn't stop to find out. When he touched home Eduardo nearly knocked him down coming right behind him.

DK was in the umpire's face, screaming something about time out and rain delay, and of course, I could see his point, but, personally, I would have been happy to go on playing in the rain, since it seemed to improve our chances. But the girls were already running off to the cars, and the crowd was scrambling for shelter, so it seemed we might as well take a rain delay.

DK wasn't satisfied with this. "We've played seven innings. That's enough to qualify for a win," he argued.

Luckily, Art isn't the type who likes to be told how to do his job. "Cool off," he said. "Play will resume when the storm passes. Unless you want to forfeit now?" And with that, he trotted off to the parking area while DK raged to the skies in the manner of King Lear. Seriously, if he weren't such a soulless oaf, I would encourage DK to look into amateur theatricals. Another time, perhaps.

For now, I jogged to the good old truck, wrenched the door open, and leapt inside. I had stashed a fat reefer under the seat, and it seemed to me that this thunderstorm was fate's way of saying, "Have a toke, Duggie. You've earned it."

However, in my vision of this plan, I was alone, or at most, sharing the smoke with Randall. I hadn't budgeted for pompoms.

Yet there they were, strewn across the dashboard like unruly sea urchins. And where there are pompoms, it follows there are cheerleaders. Or, in this case, Phoebe, my own personal pep squad.

"Oh Duggie, isn't this great! You're doing it! You're going to beat them, I can just feel it!" She threw her skinny arms around my neck and kissed my cheek, and, I have to admit, it didn't feel bad. But, I couldn't encourage this girlish glee. I removed her arms from around me and tried to establish a little neutral ground between us. Luckily, just then I heard the familiar clicking of Rufie's nails on the window behind me. He was standing on his hind legs, soaking wet and looking to join the party. I might have hesitated but that it struck me as the perfect dampener, the dog *ex machina* so to speak. I opened the door on my side, and he clambered in, scrabbling his way across me to the space between me and Phoebe, where he sat panting with an aroma of wet dog fur guaranteed to douse any notions of romance.

I smiled brightly at Phoebe. "He's afraid of thunder," I explained.

She nodded gamely. "Poor baby," she said.

I reached under the seat for the joint. My lie about Rufie—he couldn't care less about thunder—had given me the perfect cue for lie number two. "I hope you don't mind, but marijuana smoke is the only thing that works to calm him down. I keep some in the truck just in case he needs it. You don't mind do you?" I waggled the joint with an apologetic shrug.

Phoebe's frowned. "But what about the game? Won't that be bad for you?"

I shook my head with a little knowing smile. "Nah. This is really mild," I lied. "It'll just calm Rufie down. Don't worry about me. Besides, it'll probably be another hour before we start playing again. This stuff'll wear off by then. Would you like some?" I lit the joint and held it out to her.

Phoebe shook her head. "I don't think so. I have to stay sharp for cheering. I tried it in college, but it made me forget what I was supposed to be doing."

"Ah. You get used to that," I said, inhaling deeply.

Phoebe looked puzzled. I exhaled with a choke and clarified. "There's nothing to be worried about. It's all in your head. Or my head. Anyway. It's a head thing. Not a genuine danger, if you get what I mean. Do you?"

She shook her damp curls again, but this time she was smiling. "You're such a nut, Duggie!"

I quailed before her renewed warmth. If Rufie hadn't been planted between us, I think she might have made another grab at me. This always happens when I get stoned. I have trouble toning down my natural charm. A girl like Phoebe, already so susceptible, well, with emotions running high as a result of the game, it's to be expected.

I glanced out the windshield and thought I saw a rainbow on the horizon. I put it down to hallucination, but a moment later Phoebe piped up and said, "Oh look! A rainbow! It's a sign!"

I wasn't so sure. So often signs are in the eye of the beholder. If you've ever studied any history you can't help noticing how many seriously wrongheaded people at one time or another made poor decisions because of the delusion that God was on their side. I'm not sure He takes sides, really.

However, sign or not, there was no question that the clouds seemed to be clearing up rather quicker than I had expected. Beams of sunlight were sparkling on the puddles, and people were starting to wander back to the field.

I wondered if I should. On the one hand, the game needed to be finished. But, on the other, I was feeling pretty wasted. Phoebe, in contrast, seemed fully charged and eager to cartwheel. Sunshine has this effect on some people, I've noticed. She bounced on her seat and said, "Come on, Duggie! Let's go kick their butts!"

"You go ahead. I'll be right along," I said, adding to my list of lies. In truth I was thinking that a short, five-minute lie-down on the seat of the truck might be just what the doctor ordered. I let Rufie out when Phoebe left and shut the door and reclined on the bench seat. Five minutes. No more.

All right. Perhaps it had stretched into ten. I don't know. But that was still no reason for Jenny to shout. "Duggie! What the hell? We've been calling you for ten minutes! Get your ass out of there! The game's already started again!"

I grabbed my glove and scuttled out the door, surreptitiously wiping the drool from the corner of my mouth. My head was spinning a bit, but I was sure it would stop once I'd been standing for a few minutes. I stood in the hot sunshine and wondered if it was just me or did the air feel a bit thick? Steam was rising from the wet grass. I looked out at the field and saw Photon coming up to bat.

"What did I miss?" I asked quietly.

Jenny snorted. "Darren struck out."

"That's it?"

"No. Witty bunted and got on base. But the pirates have jumped ship."

"What do you mean?"

"What do you think I mean? They're not shooting." She frowned and tilted her head to the sidelines. "And I think that might be why."

I looked where she was pointing, and my stomach did a quick back flip. Sheriff Quayle was leaning against his cruiser, with his sunglasses on, looking altogether too happy. Not that I have anything against him as a fellow human. But, the man has a master's degree in the persecution of harmless hippies, and the sight of him was always a major bringdown in the best of circumstances. If Mindy's brother had seen Quayle, that would explain the suspension of pirate attacks. Which meant we had to deploy some other strategy. And fast. In the few minutes we had been talking Photon had self-destructed in a blaze of manic swinging and colorful obscenities which got laughs from some in the crowd, but not from his teammates.

I hurried over to the bench. On my way there a tiny hand grabbed my arm, and I almost snapped at the grabbee, thinking it was Phoebe again. Then I focused on the female face and recognized Mindy.

"Duggie!" she whispered.

"Yes?" I hissed impatiently.

"I think my brother bailed."

"I noticed."

"But I have an idea. Want to hear it?"

"No. There's no time. Just do it. Surprise me. We need a miracle."

She patted me on the shoulder, and her eyes twinkled as she said, "Cheer up. I've got a pair."

I hustled to the bench. We had two outs. It was the bottom of the eighth. Jenny was coming up to bat. I glanced back at the Sheriff and saw that he was talking to Kevin, the weasel who abandoned the team without a word of explanation. Seeing the two of them together reminded me of something. I couldn't think what. But I didn't have time to think about it now. I folded my arms and braced for the next pitch.

I think, when I consider all the unusual momentum shifts of that long day, the one that followed might be my favorite. At least in the top five.

Nunley started his windup as usual. His knee went up, he turned his body, and then, just as he was bringing his arm around to unleash what no doubt would have been another strike, Mindy unveiled her secret weapons.

She was standing on the sidelines right where her former boyfriend's gaze couldn't miss her, and she was flashing two of the most beautiful breasts I have ever seen. Not that I've seen that many, in person, mind you. But, as they say in real estate, it's all about location, location, location, and those beautiful breasts were in the right place at the right time to take the air right out of Nunley. He served up a floating cream puff for Jenny, and she clobbered it. Plus, when she ran to first, the infielders were similarly distracted by Mindy's display, so, by the time the curtain fell on the show, Witty had advanced to third, Jenny was on first, and Rosalie was up next.

You could tell by her face that she understood the gravity of the situation. We were still trailing by five runs. Even if she somehow miraculously knocked the ball into the stratosphere, we would need two more just to pull even. And we would have to keep them from scoring any more. I felt a momentary rush of relief that I was so stoned that I no longer really cared.

Just then something yanked my arm and I turned curiously, half-hoping to see Mindy in full flash mode. The face at my elbow wasn't hers. It was Glory, and her face was redder than usual, her eyes blazing with the old familiar fury of an older sister about to scorch a sibling.

"You brainless twit! Where have you been?" She leaned closer and sniffed my shirt, a clear violation of personal space, but I was too ripped to complain.

"Oh, out and about," I replied, attempting airy joviality.

"Don't give me that crap! You've been getting high while the whole game is going down the toilet!"

I weighed this. "Does it really matter?"

She punched my shoulder and got a hold of my collar, pulling me closer. "Listen, you ninny! If you don't win this game, Eduardo going's to leave me for Shitley, and that's going to be the end of the café and the end of your job and what's more, I will personally make your life a living hell."

"Ah. So. It matters. To you."

"It should matter to you if you had half a brain!"

I frowned slightly. It was clear that she was upset, but there was no need to get personal. Still, I could see her point. I looked past her to where Rosalie had attempted to swing at the first pitch and lost her grip on the bat. It sailed out toward the infield and nearly clipped Nunley. For a second I mused that perhaps this was a tactic worth pursuing. But then I thought she probably wouldn't be able to hit him if she tried.

Off to the sideline Phoebe's cheerleaders were lining up. There was no reason to despair just yet.

I raised my chin and patted Glory on the back. "Don't worry, sis. We've got a few tricks left."

She glared at me and opened her mouth, no doubt to make some insulting remark, but, whatever it was, I never found out, because just as Nunley was beginning his windup the cheerleaders launched into a new and thrilling routine.

"Give me an M!" They shouted as one of them bent over and mooned the pitcher.

"Give me an O!" Another adorable girl added her shining posterior to the line.

"Give me another O!"

You get the picture. It was breathtaking. Nunley didn't even try to pretend he wasn't staring. By the time they added the "N" everyone on the field was so mesmerized that Rosalie, waiting at the plate for the pitch, became vexed and yelled, "Hey!" And at this, Nunley seemed to remember where he was and tossed the ball toward the plate without giving it the full measure of his attention, which allowed Rosalie to pour all her vexation into hitting the ball, which, amazingly, she did. It wasn't a textbook hit, by any means, but it took some funny bounces and slipped by the infielders and that was enough to let Rosalie scamper to first while Witty and Jenny scored.

The cheerleaders straightened up and screamed enthusiastically.

Nunley stood on the mound fuming. DK came over and they had a quick meeting, involving a lot of flailing arms and finger pointing. It was pleasant to watch. I was enjoying the look of frustration on their faces, when suddenly I got another jab on the shoulder. I don't know why it is that people seem to feel they have to hit me to get my attention. A simple "hey you" would be sufficient.

However, when I turned and saw it was Jenny, I quickly forgot my pain. "What's up?" I said.

"You are soon, you big dope. Do you think you can bat? Honestly Duggie. I thought you were going to stay straight for the game."

"I was. But then it rained. And I thought—"

"Never mind. I don't care what you thought. Just try not to strike out, okay?"

"I'm not up yet, though, right?"

She shook her head and looked over to the plate where Babe was swinging her bat in a menacing way.

I won't lie. Jenny's words had struck a nerve. I felt as if someone had just dumped a load of gravel on my head. I was so preoccupied I turned away from the game until I heard the sound of Babe's hit and looked up to see her sliding into second. Rosalie was on third. And I was up.

Well, you know how it is when someone says, "don't look down" and suddenly you can't stop yourself?

I stood at the plate, and all I could hear in my head were the words "strike out" over and over. I tried to block it out, but when I saw Nunley rear back with the ball I had a moment of panic, and, I think, though I couldn't swear to it because it all happened fast, I think I may have closed my eyes for a second and possibly flinched just a bit. Which is funny when you think about it, because really, at the time of the first flinch, I had nothing to flinch about. Yet, a heartbeat later a rocket of pain shot through my side, and I fell to the ground, flinching like there was no tomorrow.

My first thought was that I'd been shot. But, feeling my side I quickly realized I was still intact and a likelier explanation presented itself. I'd been struck by the pitch. I got up foggily and looked around and noticed that everyone was staring at me expectantly. Then Art gave me a shove and said, "Go to first, moron."

I glanced over at our bench and saw that Jenny was applauding, so I figured it could have been worse. My ribs felt as if I'd been kicked by a horse, but at least I hadn't struck out. Not only that, but I was on base and Randall was coming up.

This was good. But, considering that we still needed to score at least two runs, I wondered if it would be good enough. Randall started off with two fast foul tips and it looked like he was about to go out with a bang, but on the next pitch he connected for a bouncing line drive that eluded the grasp of the first baseman and continued on into the wilds of right field. Rosalie ran for home and I took off. As I reached second I glanced back to see if the ball was on its way, and that's when I saw Chumley. I never saw a Great Dane look more angelic.

Technically Chumley is owned by Garth Padgett, owner of the Hardware n' More store in town, but most people give Chumley the edge in the relationship, and even Garth admits that for the most part, whatever Chumley wants, Chumley gets. So it was with great delight that I saw that what he wanted at the moment was the ball, which he had picked up, and was playing a game of keepaway with the shortstop and a couple of outfielders. The ball looked like a pea lodged in his capacious slobbering jaws, and he was darting back and forth, clearly enjoying himself. I uttered a silent prayer to the god of monstrous dogs and ran on, touching third and continuing to homeplate. There I turned to watch the show, but, unfortunately, as Chumley made no distinction between our players and theirs, he had, in the course of his zigging and zagging, zagged right into Randall and decked him, and the Sandblasters took advantage of the turn of events to pile onto him and hold him in place while they tricked Chumley into coughing up the ball by offering him a Slim Jim. Thus the inning ended with the score tied.

The Sandblasters came in, grunting and banging their gloves, while we took the field, knowing we had to stop them from scoring another run if we were to have any hope at all.

CHAPTER 11

vitam regit fortuna non sapienta
Chance, not wisdom, governs human life.

So there we were. Top of the ninth and dead even, with the Sandblasters coming up to bat.

On the face of it, it was doable. All we had to do was hold them for one more at bat, and then slip one run by them on our turn.

But, when I considered our arsenal of tricks, it seemed fairly well depleted. We had used nudity, violence, guile, and wild dogs, and still the Sandblasters hadn't crumbled. I was wishing I had thought to offer them some special brownies during the break when a disturbance in the Force caught my eye, and I looked over at what appeared to be a small dust storm in the vicinity of the Sandblasters' bench.

Then I reasoned that dust storms don't generally shout things like "screw you" and "get bent" as this particular storm was doing. Suddenly the truth hit me. It was no ordinary dust storm. Apparently, during the rain delay, DK's team hadn't spent the time relaxing and hydrating. Instead they had started bickering among themselves, and judging by the fragments of invective floating from their melee, some of them had made other plans for the day, in anticipation of what they naturally had expected would be a swift victory. Now they were getting impatient with how long the game was taking, and they were turning on each other, growling and snapping like a pack of hyenas debating the division of a dead zebra.

I chuckled with delight. You can never count on the Fate card turning things your way, but, as I watched one pumpkin-headed goon raise his hammy fist and clobber one of his teammates, I thought things were definitely looking up.

The scuffle only lasted few minutes before DK, as alpha ape, asserted himself and put down the insurrection. But you could tell they weren't the same carefree marauding interlopers. They'd had enough of Rapidan County.

Hah! I thought. Now we just need to give them that little bit more that makes all the difference.

I was puzzling over how to do this when a hard kick on my shin refocused my thoughts. "Hey, what was that for?"

"I've been calling your name for like ten minutes!" It was Mindy.

"Surely not ten?"

"Okay, maybe five. But long enough. And we don't have time to waste."

"Agreed." I nodded tensely. This petite schemer had come through in the past. I hoped she had one more miracle up her sleeve. Although, of course, she had no sleeves at the moment, but, you know what I —

"Duggie! Are you listening?"

I shook myself. "Yes. What's the plan?"

She leaned closer and lowered her voice. In a few well chosen words she outlined a last ditch strategy that might enable us to hobble the Sandblasters for one final inning. Apparently, though his fellow snipers had fled the scene, brother Andrew hadn't hung up his paintball gun just yet, and had wedged himself under a car parked well within firing distance of homeplate. With a few pinpoint shots, Mindy's scofflaw sibling could potentially give us the edge we desperately needed. I gave her the thumbs up and she skipped off.

I decided against sharing the news with the team, though, because I didn't want them counting on anything. Even if we did manage to stop DK's gang from scoring, we still had to score in order to win, and we would need a major transfusion of luck to do that.

However, from the moment DK stepped to the plate, it seemed that whatever fumes of luck we had been driving on had vanished. I had hoped that the quarreling on the sideline might have diminished the Sandblasters death squad efficiency. This did not appear to be the case. If anything, they seemed to be even more deadly when angry. DK started things off by banging a home run on the first pitch. The only good thing you could say about this was that at least there was no one on base so they were only up by one more run. But then the next goon up hit a triple, and the one after him hit a double.

I looked over to Mindy and caught her eye. She nodded, and I waited for a miracle.

Brick Nunley was at the plate, cocking his bat, and grinning at Jenny. She rolled her eyes in disgust and then hurled the ball toward the plate. Nunley got as far as bringing the bat around when something caught him just below the crotch. A bright orange splat of paint left no doubt as to what had happened, but, though Nunley roared in protest, Art refused to stop play. He offered Nunley the choice of forfeiting or continuing.

Well, you might think that wouldn't be enough to turn the tide, but it's funny how being shot in a sensitive region will take a man's mind off the job in hand. Nunley couldn't keep his eye on the ball after that. He struck out, and made the mistake of taking his frustration out on Art, poking him in the chest and shouting about dirty tricks. Art told him to shut up or he'd throw him out of the game.

Nunley didn't. And Art did.

Heartwarming as this turn of events was, we didn't fully appreciate the repercussions of it until after we managed to get the other two outs, with the help of Andrew's stellar marksmanship. By that time the Sandblasters had a comfortable four run lead, and the sheriff's men were down on the ground trying to pull Andrew out from under a Chevy Impala. We gave him a standing ovation as they led him off the field.

Then it was down to us. We gathered for one last huddle, and I urged them all to fight for the honor of Rapidan, and Photon sniggered and told me to have another toke. But I didn't mind. The important thing was, we still had a chance, and even better, because with Nunley thrown out of the game the Sandblasters had to put in a different pitcher, and we had hopes that he might be more hittable.

At first, this looked to be the case. Eduardo was first up, and he hit a homer on the first pitch. Nice as this was, all I could think was how much nicer it would have been if we'd had the bases loaded. But, of course, it never pays to wallow in what might have been. Especially when the next man up was Darren, who hadn't gotten a hit all day.

As he slouched over to the plate Darren nudged me and whispered, "I'm 'onna try what you did."

I stared after him completely fogged. What, I wondered, had I done that was worth emulating? Within seconds the mystery was solved as I watched Darren lean forward into the pitch, turning his back slightly so that the ball caught him on the ribs. "Ooof," he yelled. Then he dropped the bat and grinned at me as he trotted to first.

I shook my head, but on reflection I realized that to a kid like Darren getting nailed by a softball probably didn't even register as something to be avoided.

Witty was up next, and you could tell he had no plans to follow Darren's lead. He swung mightily at the first two pitches and clipped both of them for high fouls. Then, on the third pitch he hammered the ball out of sight, driving in Darren and himself. Suddenly we were only one run behind again.

The cheerleaders took it up a notch, and the crowd was on their feet chanting "Moon Light! Moon Might!" I looked through the crowd and saw even Glory was yelling her head off.

Then momentum hit a snag when Photon came up to bat. You could tell by the steam coming out of his ears and the crackle of sparks coming off his hair that he wanted to light the fuse that would blow the game apart. But, a whiff of his breath as he lurched past told me that his internal guiding mechanism was pickled in José Cuervo, and his swings, though wild and lusty and full of the will to win, failed to come anywhere close to the actual ball.

Jenny was next. She had had a rough day so far, especially that last round with the Sandblasters tearing up the bases. The crowd got quiet as she went into her stance. She let the first two pitches go by without a swing, even though Art called one of them a strike. But Jenny got what she wanted on the third pitch. She hit it cleanly, a line drive into centerfield that nearly took the pitcher's head off. He ducked to avoid being hit while Jenny arrived safely on first.

Then Rosalie was up, and three pitches later she was out. But this was okay, I thought, because Babe was up next. At least I thought it was okay. I hadn't accounted for the Sandblasters stooping to strategy. In a way, I guess you could say this was evidence of a moral victory, that the enemy which had planned to annihilate us with mere brute force had been compelled to revise its plan. They intentionally walked Babe, leaving us with two outs and the winning runners on base. And I was up next.

My legs stopped functioning as I felt the eyes of everyone in the stands turn on me. Normally, I enjoy being the center of attention, and can always be relied upon to entertain and amuse with the well-chosen anecdote or pithy Latin axiom. But at this critical moment it dawned on me that not only was the team counting on me, but so was my sister, and, in fact, the very existence of the Moonlight Café might depend on the outcome of this game. My throat closed up, and I tried to swallow my nerves as I shuffled toward the plate.

I was trying hard not to look at Jenny and Babe, both of them waiting out there for me to do something heroic. I knew I needed to focus on the job. But in my head Jenny's voice kept saying "don't strike out," and my hands were sweating so much I had trouble holding onto the bat.

Then, before I turned to face the pitcher, I got this spooky twinge in my neck, and I glanced over to the crowd, and my heart nearly stopped when my eyes met the Sheriff's. He was staring at me the way a snake looks at a rat the second before swallowing it. I blinked and shook my head, and tried to tell myself I was just being paranoid, but it was no good. I felt as if a cold clammy hand had just reached inside my chest and started squeezing the life out of me.

I forced myself to turn away and suddenly, fwap! "Strike one," I heard Art say.

I stepped away from the plate and took some deep breaths.

"Come on, Duggie! You can do it!"

Even in my dazed state I recognized Phoebe's star-struck tone. I gripped the bat tighter, squared my shoulders, and stepped back for the next pitch. I saw it coming, big as a basketball, and I swung as hard as I could, sure that this was going to be the magical moment of which every boy dreams.

And yet. Next thing I knew, Art was announcing, "Strike two." So much for magical moments.

The next pitch bounced in the dirt, and luckily I checked my swing before it got there, so I was still alive. But, the sense of peril loomed like a Kansas tornado, black and swirling, bearing down on me with the inevitability of a Hollywood disaster flick.

When the next pitch came, I felt the whole world slow down as the bat left my shoulder and swung closer, closer. I could see the stitching on the ball. And then, there was nothing. Except Art saying, "Strike three."

I stood there in a widening pool of silence. From somewhere in the fog that enveloped me I heard Photon say, "Aw, shit!"

And that remark seemed to uncork the frustrations of the multitude, for suddenly the air was filled with the din of people shouting and complaining. I tried not to listen too closely, since I guessed they probably weren't singing my praises, and, though I didn't blame them, I suspected they wouldn't extend the same courtesy to me. I wondered if I could sneak away to my truck and find solace in the other half of that joint, but my plans were abruptly altered when someone grabbed my arms from behind and clamped a pair of handcuffs on my wrists.

"You have the right to remain silent," the cop began, continuing with the familiar Miranda spiel. Not that I could have managed a word at that moment. I was totally stunned. I mean, I'd let everyone down, certainly, but surely this wasn't cause for legal action? Then I caught sight of Sheriff Quayle's smug face, and noticed Kevin hiding behind him, and all of a sudden I had a bad feeling about the way this day was going. There are worse things than losing a ball game.

Quayle's men put me in the back of a patrol car, and then he got in and off we went. I was dying to know what they were arresting me for, but I had been so shocked when they put the cuffs on me that I hadn't really listened closely and now, of course, I couldn't exactly ask for details without possibly giving them information they didn't need to have. So I hunched in my seat and waited to see what developed, taking the *sile et philosophus esto* course. "Be silent and be a philosopher," good advice any time.

At first, no one said anything. Judging by the route we were taking, we were heading out of town. Gradually, I realized we were driving toward the mountain. My mountain. It was cool in the air-conditioned car, but I started to sweat. No wonder Kevin had quit the team. No wonder he wouldn't look me in the eye. I started making feverish plans for how I would skip the country once I got out on bail. But what if they didn't let me out on bail? Oh god, oh god, oh god!

By the time they stopped the patrol car in front of my shack I had gone through the seven stages of grief. Or is it five? No matter. This was it. The end. No bookstore for me. No happily ever after with Jenny somehow in the rosy colored future perfect. For me the cold gray prison with some dour cellmate who would demand more affection than I honestly had it in me to give. I stared glumly out the car window at a future that held no appeal whatsoever.

"Come on, Sunshine. This is your hippie home right? Let's see what you got here."

They pulled me out of the car, and I trudged behind them as they started up onto the porch.

"It's out back."

I recognized Kevin's whiney voice. He was flanked by the pair of cops who had followed the sheriff's car up the mountain. I glared at him. He motioned to his father and said, "this way," as he walked around the back of the house and into the woods, leading them straight to the bus.

"Come on, loser," one of the cops said to me, shoving me in the back. I stumbled forward and followed the Quayle parade. When they got to the bus, the Sheriff turned and smiled at me.

"You dirtbags are all alike. You think you're so smart. Well, it's the end of the road for you, Moon. You're not going to be going anywhere for a long, long time." Quayle actually rubbed his hands like some silent movie villain as he said this, and I could understand the man's natural instinct to revel in the moment of his triumph. He climbed up into the bus with a couple of his patrolmen. I waited outside. I didn't need to go in there. I knew what they'd find.

Yet, when they came back out a minute or two later, I was surprised by the change in their expressions. The Sheriff's look of glee had been replaced by one of intense irritation, and the men behind him were scratching their heads and looking around under the bus and in the scrub nearby as if they'd lost a contact lens.

After several minutes of this the Sheriff glared at me and said, "So. I bet you think you're pretty smart."

I raised my eyebrows. I mean, of course I do think I'm fairly intelligent, but I knew the Sheriff was deploying sarcasm, which could only mean one thing. A miracle had occurred. True, The Miracle of the Softball Game had not come to pass, but if Fate wanted to substitute The Miracle of the Pot Bus, well then, I certainly wasn't about to complain. No sirreee.

But, just to see for myself, I walked over to the bus and climbed up the steps and instantly the scent hit me. It wasn't the scent I'd been expecting. Gone were the six-foot-tall sensimilla plants, and in their place were flats of basil, oregano and thyme. The whole bus smelled like a vegetarian pizzeria. I stared, my mind racing. On the one hand, great news that I was not the owner of an illegal crop. But, on the other hand, where was my pot?

I tottered out into the sunlight, blinking and dazed. One of the cops came over and took off the handcuffs. The Sheriff was still staring at me, and Kevin was whining at him about how he had seen the pot, and it had been there, and he wasn't making it up etc., etc. Sad, really.

After a few more minutes of beating the bushes and kicking at the bus tires the representatives of Rapidan's legal force called it a day, got back in their cars and left without a word of farewell or apology for having impugned my character. I guess they knew it was the sort that could withstand a certain amount of impugning without lasting damage.

At any rate, they were gone, and I, for one, wasn't sorry. Except for losing the game. As that thought bobbed back to the top of the charts I went over to the porch and sat down to contemplate the bigger picture. It didn't look good.

I wondered where my cash crop had gone and if I would ever find out. I wondered if Eduardo would really quit the café. I wondered if Glory would lose her business as a result. I didn't wonder if I would be fired. I took that as a given. But I did wonder whether Jenny would ever forgive me for striking out.

While I sat there, rubbing my chafed wrists (those handcuffs aren't exactly designed for comfort), lost in thought, I became aware of a rhythmic panting sound that moments later materialized in the form of Rufie, slobbering happily in my face as if he, at least, accepted me with all my failings.

"How did you get here?" I murmured as I hugged him.

"I gave him a ride."

My heart stopped. Jenny was standing over me, sunlight glinting on her shoulders, where the wings would be if there were any justice in this world.

"Thanks."

She sat down next to me and gave me a look which I couldn't read. I couldn't tell if she was mad or sad or some cocktail of both. Then she shook her head and smiled. "You idiot," she said.

Well, that was fair.

"I'm sorry about losing the game," I said.

She nodded. "I know. It's okay." She patted my knee. "Everything's gonna be okay."

I didn't see how this could be so, but it felt so good to hear her say it, even if it was a complete lie, that I wished I could wrap myself up in those words and forget all the trouble I was in. But I felt I had to be a man, so I said, "I don't think everything can be okay anymore. If Eduardo leaves the restaurant—"

"He's not going to."

"He's not?"

"Nope. I had a chat with Glory, and suggested that if she hired Marilyn to work at the bar she could guarantee that Eduardo would never leave."

I stared at her. I'd always known she was an angel, but I saw now that even that was underestimating Jenny's powers.

"That's great! So Glory's not mad?"

"Not so much. It's too bad the Sandblasters won, but at least Shipley didn't, and that was the important thing. Who cares about those other jerks?"

I nodded. "Right." I paused, absorbing this great good news. But then, as it sunk in, the other, not so great news reared its ugly head, and I didn't know if I should mention it, since Jenny had never approved of the plan.

I frowned a bit, and I guess she noticed, because she said, "Something else bothering you?"

I hesitated. Then I decided I had no right to hold back anything from this angel of mercy, so I told her about Quayle's visit and the missing pot. "So, I guess I'm not going to make any money after all, and I won't be able to open the bookstore, and I don't know how I'm going to pay your sister and—"

I stopped because, again, she had patted my knee, and I'm not made of steel. I looked into her eyes and was surprised to see little embers of amusement in them.

"Duggie? Didn't you notice anything funny about the bus?"

"Funny?"

"Yeah. You didn't notice that the windows weren't covered? Or that the lights inside were different?"

I frowned. In my haste, perhaps I hadn't looked as closely as I might have. I was so shocked at what wasn't there, I guess I overlooked what was.

"Um, no. Now that you mention it, I didn't even notice that. But ... the lights were different. And ... how did you know?"

She smiled and put her arm around my shoulders and squeezed, and of course then I missed the next few things she said, but, when my head cleared I heard her say, "So Morris called Eric, and he arranged for one of his landscape guys to fill another school bus with herbs, and Morris drove your bus to a safe place, and Eric replaced it with the other one."

"So Morris—"

"He's got your pot."

"But how did he know?"

"I told you. When Amanda told me that Mindy had been talking to Kevin, I suspected that little rat was up to no good. Then when he didn't show up for that game, I told Morris, and he said he would take care of it."

"But why didn't you tell me?"

"Duggie. You've had a lot on your mind these past few weeks, and we just thought it would be better if we didn't add to your worries."

"Well, yeah, but—"

"And everything's gonna be fine now." She smiled at me as she said this, so I couldn't really complain. I mean, yes, if, on that ride in the sheriff's car, I had known the surprise that awaited them, I would have been spared a lot of mental anguish. But now, with Jenny at my side, and my pot crop somewhere safe, and Glory happy with Eduardo locked in on the kitchen staff, and Witty free to woo Rosalie, well, the list of happy endings seemed long enough to offset the mere loss of a softball tournament.

"I guess you're right. It's all worked out for the best," I said.

But Jenny frowned and shook her head, and my heart, which had been rising like a hot air balloon on all this good news, sank.

"I don't know, Duggie. This whole thing with you nearly getting yourself locked up and sent away for who knows how long has made me think. I mean, Morris does what he can, but he can't be with you every minute of the day."

"Oh," I said. "So. What do you suggest?"

"I know you love your privacy out here on the mountain, and I know you're happy alone, but I'm beginning to think you need closer supervision."

I stared at her, unable to follow the drift. Did she think I needed a roommate? There was a twinkle in her eye that was making it hard for me to think clearly, and I might have sat there indefinitely with my mouth hanging open if she hadn't continued.

"I was thinking maybe I should check up on you more often."

"Really?" I croaked.

"Would you mind if I came over every day? And maybe some nights? Just to make sure you're not playing with matches or wrestling bears or whatever crazy idea occurs to you next?"

My heart was pounding like a jackhammer. "Well, if you're sure," I said.

She smiled and I couldn't stop myself. I put my arms around her and kissed her, and it was the kiss of my dreams, the good ones, the ones where her lips melt against mine and the world dissolves into this misty pink haze, and there may be birds singing in the distance, but I couldn't swear to that, I only know that that happy moment was as close to heaven as I ever expect to get.

When the kiss ended I asked, "Are you sure you won't get tired of me?"

And then she laughed and said, "Oh Duggie, for a smart guy sometimes you're such a dope."

After she had gone, I sat on the porch musing *more meo*, in my fashion, on the strange and wondrous turn of events. And, so astounded was I by this most recent development that it was some time before my thoughts returned to the disappearance of my cash crop. I wondered where, exactly, Morris had parked the pot bus.

Obviously, I trusted Morris. I mean, he'd saved my neck and all. But, still.

I wondered if he fully appreciated the responsibility of caring for the plants in the crucial final stages.

Knowing his distaste for tangling with the law, I doubted that he would have parked the bus at his house, but, where could it be?

I tried calling him, but he didn't answer, and, of course, I couldn't leave a message. I was at the point of walking up to his house and waiting for him to show up, when he came ambling out of the woods and onto my porch.

He gave me a stern look. "The sheriff gone?"

I nodded. "They're all gone." I hesitated, eager to raise the topic of the absent bus, but, wanting to do so tactfully.

"Thank you for saving my skin," I said.

"Somebody had to." He sat down beside me and said, "I trust you've learned something from all this."

"You can say that again."

"I trust you've learned something from all this."

I smiled, and waited for him to tell me all. But, in his usual maddening way, Morris seemed content to take in the scenery while I supplied the conversation.

"Say," I said, after another empty minute, "I'm curious. How did you know the sheriff was coming, anyway?"

Morris shook his head. "When your little friend Kevin failed to show up on the field yesterday, I guessed that he was up to no good. I went home and came up here through the woods, and saw him coming out from behind your house, looking far too pleased with himself. I didn't know if he'd go straight to his father or try to blackmail you first, but when he didn't come back to the game, I knew we had to work fast."

I nodded. "Yes. Well, again, I can't thank you enough. But, why didn't you tell me? I mean, all's well that ends well, and all that, but, that ride up here in the sheriff's car? With him and Kevin gloating all the way? Not the best time of my life."

Morris smiled. "I wish I could have seen their faces when they came out of the bus."

"That *was* sweet." My heart warmed at the memory. "But I still don't understand why you couldn't have let me in on the plan."

"There wasn't time. And we thought it best that you know nothing, in case they interrogated you."

"You think I would have cracked under pressure?"

Morris shrugged.

I frowned and considered this. I don't enjoy pain, of course. And it's entirely possible that Quayle and his men might have expressed their disappointment with brutish force. Unlikely, but possible. I relaxed the frown.

"All right then. I guess I can see your reasoning. But where's the bus?"

"Ahh. About that."

I frowned anew.

"You didn't get rid of the bus?"

"No."

"So where is it?"

Morris was silent for a long minute. "It's on its way to a far, far better place."

"Where?"

"It's best that you not know."

"But ... but ... I have to cut it, dry it, bundle it—"

Morris held up his hand. "Duggie, there will be no cutting, drying or bundling for you."

"But ... but—"

"No buts, Duggie. The sheriff will be watching every move you make for the rest of the summer. This crazy scheme almost got you locked up once. You should be thankful that the contraband is gone."

I gaped at him. "Gone? What do you mean, gone? I thought Jenny said you'd moved it to a safe place."

"We did. It's on its way to a medical marijuana clinic in Oregon, where there's no law against it."

"But what about my profit?"

Morris shook his head. "I think you can profit from the lessons learned in this whole experience."

"But, but—"

"It's over. You're going to have to straighten up and fly right. At least until this blows over."

I leaned back in my chair, stunned.

"What about my bookstore?"

"You'll have to come up with a new plan. I'd suggest something *not* illegal."

I frowned at him. Easy for him to be sarcastic at my expense. But now that Jenny was going to be at my side I'd need more ...

I sat back in my chair. Jenny was going to be with me. Of her own free will.

"You okay?" Morris was leaning forward, looking at me as if he were the doctor waiting to see if his patient was having a bad reaction to the wonder drug.

Jenny wanted to be with me. As the possibilities of this new development expanded in my soul I felt as if I were high, but without the familiar confusion. It was all clear to me now.

True, the bookstore plan might not happen as originally mapped out. But weighed against this was the irrefutable solid gold fact that Jenny might at this very moment be packing a few things and ...

Reflecting on this, I felt the natural instinct to celebrate with a pleasant smoke. I got up to get my stash from inside.

As I opened the screen door Morris said, "Don't bother."

I stopped with my hand on the door. "What do you mean?"

"Tell me this: if the Sheriff had had the presence of mind to search your house, what would he have found?"

I stepped away from the door. "My stash?"

"Did you think he couldn't find it?"

"I never thought he'd look."

"But, since he was here ..."

"I see your point. He could have ransacked the place."

"Or planted something."

I sat back down. "I never thought of that."

Morris lifted his eyebrows slightly. "Think about it now."

After another minute I said, "So ... did you take my stash?"

"Let's just say your stash is also in a safe place."

"But ... but ..."

"You'd like to get stoned now?"

"Are you saying you have my pot?"

"Are you saying you'd like to smoke some?"

"Do you have my stash?"

"Do you need to know?"

"Can you just give me a straight answer?"

"Is that what you really want?"

I sighed. "You know what I want."

"Are you sure?"

I had to smile. You can't beat him.

"Yes, please," I said. "Light it up and pass it here."

THE END

ABOUT THE AUTHOR

Born a stone's throw from Lake Erie, C.H. Sprague lived for many years in the foothills of Virginia's Blue Ridge Mountains, where the Duggie Moon stories unfold. *Potluck* is the first in the series, which continues in *Moon's Blues*. A third Duggie adventure is in the works.

As Constance Sprague, she also writes fiction about escape artists and green magic. Her novels include *Alice and The Green Man*, a gardener's fantasy, *Tall Order*, a Montlake romance, and *The Greening*, an environmental fantasy trilogy.
www.chsprague.com

www.ingramcontent.com/pod-product-compliance
Lightning Source LLC
Chambersburg PA
CBHW050950120626
46552CB00001B/468